A SMALL APOCALYPSE

A SMALL APOCALYPSE

Stories

LAURA CHOW REEVE

TriQuarterly Books / Northwestern University Press
Evanston, Illinois

TriQuarterly Books
Northwestern University Press
www.nupress.northwestern.edu

Printed in the United States of America

10 9 8 7 6 5 4 3 2 1

ISBN 978-0-8101-4694-5 (paper)
ISBN 978-0-8101-4695-2 (ebook)

Cataloging-in-Publication Data are available from the Library of Congress.

For Ace & Rodeo—
who helped me feel brave in the apocalypse

Contents

A SMALL APOCALYPSE

Milked Snakes

She unpacked the revelation like a souvenir from her suitcase. Cell service had been bad at the conference outside Atlanta, but in brief moments of honesty with herself, Beth knew that she didn't want to talk to him, that she hadn't missed him.

"We need to talk," she told him.

"Shit."

"It's not bad," she said. "I don't think it's that bad."

"OK."

They were in their shared bedroom, one of seven in a three-story house in West Philadelphia. Beth had found the house with a friend and soon there were seven humans, three cats, and a dog living in it. When someone kicked a hole in the wall, her boyfriend stuffed it with a pair of his underwear, saying he'd fix it more permanently soon. Now the room was cold, and she had to put a second sweatshirt over her first to stop shivering.

"When are you going to fix the wall?" she asked him. He was generally handy. She had only been living on her own for a year when they started dating; he was almost ten years her senior.

She didn't mean for it to happen, but it was easier to have him cook them dinners and fix leaking sinks, loose doorknobs.

"Is that all you want to talk about?" Relief moved through him and she could see him release the tension in his neck and jaw.

"No," Beth said. "Sorry."

They'd met at a house show in South Philadelphia. Her ex-boyfriend's band was playing, and she was pretending not to care. She shared a six-pack of watery beer with a friend. He was cute, if in a less obvious way, and played along with her flirtatious games of touching hands and light teasing. Beth imagined he thought she was charming, something he later confirmed, and she was happy to have the distraction. He walked her to the train station, rolling his bike alongside, and they tumbled into a relationship quickly and quietly. Soon it was a year later, and they shared a bedroom and two of the house's three cats. They hung out with other punks in the neighborhood and their housemates, who cooked vegetarian meals and ate pints of Ben & Jerry's ice cream that they bought from the gas station a few blocks east of their house. Even in winter they ate pints of ice cream.

She was one foot out of this world of mostly white punk kids who played music in dusty basements and felt overly romantic about it and each other. She liked some of the music, and pretended to like the rest, because she didn't yet know of any other world in which she might place the parts of her misfit self.

"Beth," he said, bringing her back to him.

"Sorry," she apologized again. He tapped his hands on the coffee table, a nervous habit that drove her crazy. He started working his way up to a full drumbeat.

"The thing is," she started. She put her hand on top of his to quiet his restless fingers. "I think I'm, well, I'm sure I'm—" The words covered her tongue like a thick film.

He looked at her, now impatient.

"I'm changing."

"What?"

"Scales, split tongue, green skin," she said. She didn't have to say more; she already knew he had a clear picture in his mind of what she was becoming.

"What does this mean for us?" he asked. He didn't seem surprised, but his hands started to jump beneath hers again.

"Nothing," she said. "At least not right now."

His jumpy hands landed on her arms, and he held her tighter than she expected, as if he was trying to hold her in place forever. Her sleeve rode up, exposing the single green scale on her wrist, and he withdrew his hands so quickly she thought her body had burst into flames.

In the uncomfortable silence that followed, she inspected their bedspread, a new small brown streak slashed through the geometric pattern. Like a paint stroke.

"Fuck," she said. "She did it again."

He sighed. One of their cats was so overweight that she could no longer clean her own butt. She remedied this by scooting herself across the hardwood floor and, most recently, their bedspread. They had bought wipes from a specialty pet store, though neither of them was brave enough to do the job. Sprinkles was already a cat prone to grouchiness.

"I'll throw it in the wash," he said.

Once Beth's scales started to show, she felt more comfortable attending the parties. Each scale was a badge of honor to prove her belonging. It was a thing not everyone could claim, though there were a few with tattooed scales on their temples and surgically forked tongues. They were welcome too, because who were they to shut someone else out?

Most of the parties were filled with humid, cold-blooded bodies warming themselves by grinding against strangers in the dark. Heat lamps were set up in semiprivate rooms for the more introverted, bellies exposed to the red and orange lights as they lounged on couches and large floor pillows. While Beth wanted to touch and be touched, she kept her hands to herself, only platonically touching another's shoulder or hand if they were already acquainted. Her boyfriend never came with her because she never asked him to. He continued to go to punk shows and sometimes Beth would go with him, wrapping her body in scarves and sweaters and coats to protect herself from the frigid air.

While it wasn't unusual for a man to date someone like her, they had trouble adjusting. Her growing tail took up more and more of their double bed, and she kept unintentionally pushing him off the edge. Still, he got used to her scales, even growing to like them. He would trace the sprouting ones on her back and a delightful chill would run through her body.

She googled "anatomy of a reptile" to learn more about her changing body. It was like a second, more complicated puberty. She had to be careful of her search phrases because the conspiracy and fetish websites overwhelmed her. She shrank, her scales multiplied. Her body wanted to walk on both her hands and feet, but she resisted the urge as much as possible. When she walked, she looked like a tree swaying in the wind, bobbing forward and back. It was like falling asleep during class with her head up: as her hands got closer to the ground, her body would jerk itself back up straight again, waking up, catching itself.

There were a few YouTube channels and Instagram accounts that she followed, dedicated to documenting their own processes. From what she could see, everything that was happening to her was normal. She couldn't bring herself to go to a doctor, but there was a growing list of specialists. There were historical records of others and a growing population, but it was still unclear what was causing the changes. It was often blamed on non-normative behavior and lifestyle choices. Most doctors refused to see patients like her, or only saw them to poke and prod with their smooth hands and invasive questions. *Please provide a detailed description of your most recent sexual encounter. Spread your legs. This should feel cold, does this feel cold? You'll feel my touch at the entrance here, what does that feel like? On a pain scale of one to ten, how does this feel? Describe your pain. Tell me about the thing that has hurt you most. I want to know your pain so intimately that I can put it on my own body and parade it around so that people think it's mine, too.*

Their skin was textured like hers: rough one way and faintly bumpy the other, smooth, with just enough interest to keep her fingers moving. They were introduced at a mutual friend's house in the summertime. The humid heat made her the happiest she had been in months, and she noticed how they made a performance of twirling their split tongue around a plastic straw before sucking the water from their glass.

The house was on a tree-lined street, and the porch was covered. She felt a shiver go through her. She wanted to go out onto the blacktop and take off her shirt. She wanted the sun to hit the places where her skin and scales melded into a hybrid of both.

"When did you realize?" they asked her, nodding toward the pads growing on her palms and tips of her fingers.

"A few months ago," Beth said. A drink fit in her hand without any effort. Everything felt sticky. Though she hadn't tested it, she instinctively knew she could crawl up a wall if she wanted it enough.

They slithered over to her. "And?"

"And what?"

"How's it going?" They said everything in a soft tone, with a slight lisp, though not a cartoonish one.

"Weird," she said, wanting to mimic the effect, wanting to try all their mannerisms on.

"I've seen you at the parties," they said, and she nodded, acknowledging that she had seen them too. "You're a good dancer," they added.

This was a lie, and Beth smiled because she knew it. She was not a good dancer, but it was nice to have someone flirt with her. It was nice to have someone like them flirt with her. Once she realized she wanted them to flirt with her, she didn't know what to do with her hands—pads and all.

"I never see you there with anybody," they said.

"I usually come alone," she said. *My boyfriend stays at home,* she thought in her head but didn't say out loud. She didn't want him to be there, on the porch in the humidity with this person who also had scales.

They let other people move between them, separate them on the porch as they got pulled into new, less private conversations. She kept her eyes on them throughout the night, wondered if her body would start to move like theirs in a few months' time.

It's a complicated thing, not knowing if you want to be someone, or to be with them.

They stopped kissing when they realized her saliva was venomous. At first, it just made his lips tingle, a sensation that turned him on, so he'd kiss her harder and push his body deeper into hers. Then his lips cracked open and bled. For a few weeks, he would walk around with blisters on his lips and still try to kiss her goodnight. "I'm hurting you," Beth said, as she searched for home remedies for the injuries she caused.

"It's worth it," he said. "You're my girlfriend. I want to kiss you." He kissed her neck, her shoulder, her stomach; he made his way down until his head was between her thighs. She clenched them together, squeezed his head tightly.

"Beth!" he said, surprised. She had hurt him, again.

"What if I'm poisonous all over?" she asked.

He got off the bed, put on a T-shirt with a hole at the neck, and walked out of their room and into the bathroom. She could hear the sharp intakes of his breath as he cleaned the broken blister on his mouth. Her tongue, still growing and reshaping itself, licked her blisterless lips, covering them in a coat of venomous lip gloss.

"You would want to kiss me if our situations were reversed," he said. It was a statement, not a question.

"Of course," she said.

He sat on the edge of the bed, his shoulders hunched. She could see the outline of his dick through his boxer briefs, still hard.

West Philadelphia is small, and she saw them everywhere—at the co-op, at the park that sloped into a bowl where people would sit and watch dogs play, at coffee shops, at the bar above her favorite Ethiopian restaurant—despite having never noticed them before. The first few times, they waved at each other casually, then they stopped to talk for a few minutes. Eventually, they made plans to grab coffee and then drinks and then dinner.

Beth tried not to shovel injera in her mouth because she could feel their eyes on her. She hadn't eaten all day and craved the tang on her tongue. Her lips puckered around a bite smothered in lemon and peppers. A pleasurable shudder went through her body.

"This one dog I walk, Seamus, looks like an actual teddy bear," they told her as they pulled out their phone and showed her a picture of a brown toy poodle in what could only be described as a green puffy vest—"for when it's cold," they said.

"And here he is with his friend Luna." They swiped to the left and the same little toy sat patiently next to a German shepherd, a pink bow clipped into the fur between her ears.

"It seems like a fun job," Beth told them. As their friendship grew, they texted her pictures of their daily dog walks with more frequency. Her favorites were videos of a salt-and-pepper Portuguese water dog playing fetch in the rain, her curly coat straightening under the weight of the water.

"But what about when it's cold?" she asked them in between sips of flat Coke. "Since my body started changing, I can barely get myself out of bed in the winter."

"I hear that," they said. They moved closer to her, so close she could feel the cool of their breath on her cheek. Their hand hovered above her arm before swooping down and picking at a small piece of lint on her sweater. "I don't think you have a warm enough coat. Heat packs in my jacket pockets help too."

"Have you ever just thought about moving somewhere warmer?"

"Not really," they said. "I'm happy here. My people are here."

"Chills run through my whole body. My blood feels like a thick gel that makes everything numb and tingly." They put their hand on her cheek, but she didn't feel any warmth.

Beth left the house show without telling him—an "Irish good-bye" she had once heard it called, though she wasn't sure if this was an offensive term. It was a cold February night, so cold that snowfall would've felt like relief. A friend had texted her about a party only a few blocks away and while she hadn't planned on going, she found herself walking in its direction.

It was a typical Philadelphia group house, filled to the brim with couches on their third or fourth life, tapestries, and house-plants growing down from the ceiling or up from the floor. Most of the furniture had been pushed to the edges of the room to create a makeshift dance floor. She zigged and zagged through the crowded room, finding the back door in the kitchen stocked with beer.

The backyard was small and would be overgrown by spring-time. It was hard to tell how many of them there were, some of their bodies camouflaged by the dead winter plants and dark-ness. Heaters were set up around the perimeter, and a firepit in the middle of the yard spit embers into the night's cold air. Beth silently slithered up to her friend Jess, who passed her a joint when she touched her shoulder.

"Didn't know if you were going to show up," Jess said while keeping her gaze steady on the fire.

"Didn't know if I was going to come," Beth responded, inhal-ing. She already felt high, her voice dreamy and distant. She inhaled again.

"How was the show?"

"Stupid." Beth said. "Are they here?"

"Your sweetie?" Jess asked, what was left of her eyebrows raised. When Jess's hair first started to fall out, she had passed Beth a pair of clippers in a sleepy bedroom and wrapped a dirty towel around her neck. Now the scales on Jess's scalp were gleaming underneath the twinkle lights strung across the yard. She was beautiful.

"Shut up," Beth said. "I hate you."

"You love me," Jess said with a cough and passed the joint back to Beth again. It was almost done. "No, I don't think they're coming."

"Why not?" she asked, conscious of the disappointment she couldn't hide. Jess looked at Beth hard. A smirk glowed on her face.

"Shut up," Beth said.

"It's not a good idea, Beth," Jess said. She put her hand on her friend's arm, gently, but Beth could feel the pressure of her sticky palms and stickier concern.

Hey r u upstairs?
Wheredyou go?
Beth ????
Call me
K im going home
Beth! R u serious?

"Sorry," Beth said as she walked into their bedroom. It was still freezing. The hole was still in the wall, the pair of underwear still doing nothing to fix it.

"You've been apologizing a lot the past few months," he said.

"Try my whole life," Beth said with a forced laugh. He furrowed his brows, tapped his hands against his thighs.

"Where did you go?"

"Why haven't you filled the hole yet? You said you would fill the hole."

"Beth, please."

"You know I'm fucking cold. I've told you I'm fucking cold. It's like you can't think of anyone but yourself." She was yelling now.

His voice stayed steady, even. "I'm sorry you've been cold, but I want to talk about where you've been."

"I don't want to talk about that. I want to talk about why there is a fucking hole in the wall! I want you to yell back!"

He unzipped his black hoodie, put it gently on the bed, and walked out of the room. Beth heard him grab a blanket and set of sheets from the hallway closet. Heard him make a bed on the couch below her. She grabbed his hoodie and wrapped it around her body; the smell of him made her want to scream.

A friend of a friend offered to give Beth a ride down to Florida. They lived only a few miles from a wildlife sanctuary in Gainesville. They told her about the deep summer heat, about the natural springs that were seventy degrees all year round. "You can stay with me until you get on your feet," they promised.

They kept the driver's window cracked as they pulled away from the house, the heater turned up high. Sweat stains peeked out from underneath their armpits. He sat on the front steps with the rest of their roommates. It was early in the morning, but they had all tumbled out of bed to see her off.

Beth didn't shed a tear as she said her goodbyes; instead, she imagined opening her mouth, holding the Florida heat on her tongue, and swallowing it whole.

Rebecca

Grace let out a soft but audible *ugh* when the Florida humidity hit her on the jet bridge. Even in May, the thick southern climate stuck to her skin.

"Your first time in Jacksonville, honey?" asked the woman who'd sat silently next to her on the five-hour flight.

"Yeah," Grace responded.

"Hope you like it," she said, as she shoved past Grace at a surprising speed. By the time Grace reached the gate, all traces of the woman were gone.

The Jacksonville airport felt like cool relief after her short walk from the plane to the terminal; she was tempted to grab a beer at the airport bar, an impulse she rationalized as a way to keep out of the heat when really it was to calm her nerves. She'd flown over two thousand miles to meet a man from the Internet, and now that she was there, she just needed a few more minutes—an hour, tops—to get herself together.

Her phone buzzed in her hand, and a text from Max appeared on the screen: *I'm here! Can't wait to finally hold you. Text me when you land.* <3 She rushed into a bathroom and locked herself in a stall. Scrolling through three months of text messages, she looked for a reason to not go back to the counter and change her return flight home. They'd met on a dating app when he was visiting Los Angeles. They exchanged numbers but didn't meet in person. A month later, he had consumed her. She was distracted, her phone always near dying. Text messages, phone calls, video chats—a variety of technological intimacies lived at their fingertips. The first time they fucked was when he described bending her over the arm of a couch and taking her from behind. After that, every vibration of her phone caused her fingers to drift down to the waistband of her jeans. There were three short bangs on the stall. "Are you okay in there?" a dismembered voice asked through the door. The voice's familiarity startled her.

"Just a minute," Grace responded.

"Come on out. A line is forming."

Grace swung the door open, but the bathroom was empty: no line, and no body to hold the voice she thought she heard. There was only her reflection and an overflowing sink. It was an automated faucet that turned on when it sensed a hand beneath it; Grace was too distracted to try and figure out how it had remained on in the empty bathroom. Her hands were still damp when she texted Max back: *Just landed! Meet you at baggage claim.*

Grace was not surprised when she finally saw him. She noticed that he'd gotten a haircut, a style meant for someone cooler than the man she'd been talking to. Everything else was the same but intensified: the lightness of his hair, the blueness of his eyes. His whole body was louder when it wasn't mediated by miles, satellites, and a backlit screen. He opened his arms when he spotted her and drew her into his chest. He smelled comfortable. She closed her eyes, ready for reassurance to flush through her. "You're finally here," he said. She nodded. She thought about the bag she'd checked, the pain in her neck, her increasing hunger.

"How does it feel to be down south?" he asked her with a laugh. He grabbed her duffel bag and strapped it to his back.

"Hot," she said. She unbuttoned the top button of her shirt.

"The trick is to submerge yourself in water." He smiled. "I'm excited you're here."

He led her to his car, their hands not touching. Grace brushed her bangs back once, twice, five times. She pushed strands behind her ears, then pulled them back over again. Sweat pooled at her hairline, under her nose, at the bottom of her back. Max told her that a girl had never flown across the country for him before. There were so many places he wanted to show her. "I'm hungry," she said. "Any of those places have good food?"

He took her to a multicolored restaurant with a candy shop on top. Bright plastic flowers covered the lime-green porch and oversized butterflies hung from the ceiling. Inside, black-and-white-striped wallpaper covered the dining room. "Cool?" he asked.

"Sure. What's good here?"

When the waiter came up to the table and saw Grace, she dropped her notepad and knocked over Max's water glass. "Holy shit." Her hand gripped her collar and the color in her face faded.

"What the hell, Sarah." Max's pants were soaked.

"I'm sorry, Max." She pulled a napkin out of her back pocket and pushed it onto his lap. "I just thought—" She looked back at Grace and faltered—grabbed a piece of ice out of Grace's water glass—"Sorry!"—and pressed it to the place where her jaw, neck, and ear met. "Y'all surprised me."

"How?" Max continued to dab his crotch with their napkins and ones from neighboring tables. Sarah looked back at Grace, her mouth agape.

"It's just been a long day. I'll get y'all an app, on me. What else can I get for you?"

Grace watched the whole scene with numbed amusement, like an episode of a sitcom she didn't like very much. She could hear a muted laugh track play in the back of her head. For a minute, she searched Sarah's face, curious if she would recognize her in the same abrupt way that Sarah had recognized Grace. When no one came to mind, Sarah's pretty face unknown to her, Grace let it roll off her back like ice water. It had happened before. It would happen again. Grace was one of those people who looked like other people.

After she finished her burger and most of Max's shrimp and grits, Grace felt human again. The food felt heavy in her stomach, Max's smile making each individual shrimp flip.

"Have I told you how excited I am that you're here?" he asked. She let him touch her hand. The tips of his fingertips lightly touched her open palm, tracing her life and love lines—she couldn't remember which was which.

"I'm excited too," she said.

Max lived in a little house with a large rosemary bush in the side yard. "Danny takes care of it," Max explained, as Grace fingered the plant in her hands. She picked a sprig and held it up to her nose, breathed it in.

"Rebecca planted it," said a voice behind her.

Grace had heard about Danny during her long phone calls with Max: how they'd been Rebecca's best friend, how they'd moved in after she died, how they cooked grilled cheese sandwiches at 3 A.M. Max described waking up to the smell of burnt toast but was never annoyed. Danny was short, no taller than Grace, and their hair fell in a messy mop of dark brown curls on top of their head. Their button-up shirt pulled tightly around their chest and their legs were covered with tattoos. The shrimp in Grace's stomach flipped again. She pulled at the hem of her shorts with one hand and pushed her bangs back with the other.

"Hey, I'm Grace."

"Welcome."

The house was cool and dark. The living room was large but cramped, with two couches and books stacked on the floor. Shelves on the wall held plants and ceramic bowls and figurines. Grace picked up a ceramic fox, only a little larger than her thumb, painted blue. She felt an overwhelming urge to put it in her pocket. Its whiskers and the tips of its ears were gold.

"You like Rebecca's stuff," she heard Danny say behind her. They walked over to her and took the fox. "She got it from an antique store in town," they explained, as they petted the back of the fox's head with their thumb.

"Sorry," Grace said. "I didn't realize."

"It's okay." Their eyes stayed on the blue fox, and Grace wasn't sure who they were reassuring.

"He told you about her?" they asked.

Grace nodded slowly even though they still weren't meeting her gaze. "A bit."

"Have you seen pictures of her?"

Grace shook her head, surprised by both her reluctance to speak and her impulse to lie. She had seen many photos of Rebecca. Despite what Grace suspected were his best efforts, Max could not completely scrub the internet's memory clean of her.

Danny took their phone out of their back pocket and swiped through a few pictures. Danny and Rebecca had their arms around each other, their heads touching. They were both smiling, but Rebecca didn't show her teeth. Rebecca's straight black hair fell to her chin; she wore red lipstick, her black eyeliner winged upward.

"You look good together," she told them.

"We do," Danny said, agreeing quickly. "Two queer mixed babies." They smiled, a sadder version of the one in the photo.

They looked at each other for what felt like a long moment, neither breaking eye contact. Grace almost reached for the fox in Danny's hand, as if perhaps something important would happen if they held it together. Before she could, Max broke the spell by walking into the house. He put Grace's bag on the floor, came up behind her, and wrapped his arms around her waist. Her flinch was barely visible, easily ignored. Danny put Rebecca's fox back in its original place on the shelf and turned to go back to the kitchen.

There were more books stacked underneath the only window in Max's bedroom—books on Marx and punk and an unworn copy of *The Wretched of the Earth*. Show fliers and screen-printed posters covered his walls; Grace's eyes fell on a single framed cross-stitch that proclaimed NO GODS NO MASTERS. Grace felt like she had been in this bedroom before, or like she would always walk into this bedroom, these bedrooms of these boys who liked to sleep with her.

Max reached for her waist, and Grace held herself still. His hand went up to cup her face, their foreheads touching. He breathed her in, and she knew that her skin smelled like butter and garlic and rosemary. She moved her head to kiss him first, to beat him to the punch. She could feel his eagerness in his lips, his tongue, his hands, and she waited for her own body to respond to his. When he reached for the waistband of her jeans, Grace wished it were her own hand instead. She pulled away.

"I'm sorry," she said. She was tired. She asked if she could take a shower. "I think I'm just nervous." Clean clothes and a towel were bundled in her arms.

She walked past Danny's room on her way to the bathroom. The door was open. Shelves grew behind the bed and were covered with ferns and succulents. A metal clothing rack neatly contained button-up shirts, jeans, and sweaters. A patchwork quilt lay on the partially unmade bed.

Danny's voice was behind her. "The bathroom's down the hall."

"Right," she said. Embarrassment creeped up her neck. "Thanks."

The water was cold, and Grace squealed when it first hit her skin. Her body temperature lowered, and the stickiness of the climate was washed down the drain for a moment. She felt for a bar of soap that smelled like oranges, her eyes closed under the rushing water. She washed her face, then made her way down the rest of her body. First her neck, then her armpits, then the soft curve of her belly, down to the bottom of her feet. She moved swiftly across her chest, between her legs. Everything felt electric; she was afraid of what touching these parts of her body might mean. All she could think about was Rebecca and the way her red lipstick emphasized the part in her upper lip. Grace wondered why she didn't show her teeth when she smiled.

Max had first told her about Rebecca during hour three of a four-hour phone call. They'd finally arrived at the topic of exes, and

Grace had just finished her story about leaving her boyfriend of four years when she got into a graduate school located across the country from the apartment they shared. "I didn't think twice about it," she said. "I told him that I was leaving and he wasn't coming with me." It wasn't until she'd received the acceptance letter that Grace realized she wanted a way out of the relationship.

"Your turn," she said. "Are you the asshole or is she?"

Rebecca had died a year before. They were living together when she came home from work and announced to Max that she was pregnant. "I was pissed," he said.

"Why?"

"We hadn't had sex in months," he told her. "It couldn't have been mine." But Rebecca had made it by herself. Her body had collected and multiplied cells all on its own.

"I asked her to marry me when we found out it was cancer," he whispered. "I thought it would be romantic, like a shitty movie." He told her about lighting up their living room with candles, about his grandmother's wedding ring that he resized to fit Rebecca's finger.

"She said no?"

"She told me I was a fucking idiot."

That night, Grace dreamt about Rebecca for the first time.

Grace and Max slept side by side. She could feel him pressing against her back. His breath was on her neck and his nose was in her hair. She let him stay there, let him wrap his arm around her middle. Rebecca used to let him stay there, let him wrap his arm around her middle. They both hated his breath on their neck—his warm, sweet breath that made the hair on the back of their necks stand up.

In the morning, Max was fully dressed, sitting on Rebecca's side of the bed and pushing Grace's bangs behind her ear. "I woke up and couldn't believe that you're here," he said. "It's too good to be true." Grace grabbed his hand and inspected it; she pressed her lips against his palm.

"There are a few bikes in the shed out back that you can use while I'm at work," he said. "Take whichever fits you best."

Grace went back to sleep for a few more hours, until the heat's incessant hug forced her out of bed. She opened all the windows in the house, but the thick air refused to budge. Grace stripped off her shirt and opened her arms to embrace a lonely fan in the living room.

"How'd you sleep?" Danny's voice jumped out at her, cold air rushing up her spine. She felt her bareness but didn't cover it up. They didn't seem to notice.

"Fine."

"I hope the heat didn't wake you up this morning," they said. "Our AC stopped working sometime last night."

"I slept fine," she said. Grace had actually woken up at 4 A.M., drenched in sweat and stifling a scream. She'd kicked the sheets off her legs in her sleep but it felt as if something was covering, or maybe holding on to, her feet. "What are you doing today?"

"It's my day off," they said. "Should we find somewhere cold?"

Danny and Grace each rode a bike to a small coffee shop that sold toast with miso butter in the morning and beer cocktails in the afternoon. The baristas, Ashley and Taylor, were friends of Danny's, and the three of them chatted about a party Ashley was hosting the next week. After they sat down, Grace could hear Ashley and Taylor giggle with one another about a date the night before. Grace enjoyed eavesdropping, listening to their private conversation about Taylor's date's tongue and the way he'd cleverly moved it. Flushed, Grace slurped her cool drink to compensate. From her cheeks to between her legs, her whole body had a pulse.

"What do you think?" Danny asked her.

"It's cute," she said, and then paused. "Is everyone queer here?"

"In Jacksonville?" they asked, amused. When they saw her face was pained, they added, "No, not everyone, but we try to carve out space where we can." They ran their hand through their hair, each curl quickly moving back into its original place. "I only really hang out with queers," they said. They pressed their hands to their chest, wrists limp.

The air conditioning felt good, and for the first time in twenty-four hours Grace felt relaxed. She told Danny about her life back in Los Angeles, her job at an overpriced boutique in Santa Monica, the constant folding of cashmere and soft wool, the white women who threw hundreds of dollars' worth of clothing on the floor of the dressing room and tried to return forty-dollar underwear. "I think the worst part is how my mind feels numb every night," she admitted. It was hard for her to stay awake on her long drive back to the San Gabriel Valley, red taillights blurring her vision at a slow, thirty-mile-per-hour pace. She was living with her parents again, had moved back in after finishing her master's degree in English literature without any job prospects, and hadn't figured out how to leave. The nights she made it home in time for dinner, they inquired about her future plans, what she wanted to do next. Grace didn't have the heart to tell them, she told Danny, that the only job she had applied for was a position fulfilling online orders at a sex shop in West Hollywood. They hadn't called her back.

Danny barely touched their coffee because they were too busy talking with their hands. They propped their elbows on the tabletop and made shapes like a shadow puppeteer. When they talked about their dad and their visits to the Dominican Republic, their movements were slow and big, trying to hold a whole other world, a language that made them feel shy, the movement between oceans and time. Their fingers became pointed and accusing when they mentioned their brother and how he'd stopped talking to them when they came out. Grace imagined a wolf projected on the wall—howling, snarling, and then a whimper. When the conversation landed back on Rebecca, Danny's hands moved to their arms in a hug around their body. They fingered the cuffs of their short-sleeved shirt, their hands never quite still.

Rebecca and Danny had met during their first year of college, when a group of students came together to start a club to "change the world or something," Danny said. "There were, like, five or six of us." Rebecca's hair was short, like a pixie, framing her face. She had moved from Orlando, barely escaping Mickey Mouse and Prince Charming. "Everybody loved her," Danny said. "She would plan parties and meetings and art shows. Most of the time you just felt lucky to be in her gravitational pull, to orbit around her." Grace nodded her head; she'd always wanted to be one of those people, one of those sticky-honey people who made everyone want to stay.

They parted ways after Danny showed Grace a bookstore downtown. The store resembled a small maze, and Grace missed Danny as soon as they were gone. She'd promised them she could find her way back to the house alone, but she wanted more of them—more of their stories, more of Rebecca. She wandered through the stacks, running her fingers along the books' spines for support. Eventually, she found her way back outside and then back to the house.

Most of the things in Danny's room looked like they had been Rebecca's. The closet was filled with dresses falling off hangers and boxes stuffed with blank postcards and photographs. Necklaces and purses hung from knobs and hooks attached to the walls. A sewing machine sat in the corner, surrounded by stacks of fabric and tote bags filled with scraps. The AC was still broken, but Grace's fingers felt cold. She opened drawers and searched through coat pockets. She wasn't sure what she was looking for but felt calmed as she surrounded herself with Rebecca's things. Grace's mother hated clutter, would often bring empty trash bags into her room and instruct her to get rid of what she no longer needed. She wouldn't be satisfied until Grace had filled the bags with books and clothes. Grace now saw that her mother was training Grace to control her sentimentality, her desire to hold a beloved object in her hand or reread old letters or keep a sweater that no longer fit because it recalled to her the time she'd worn it on a bike ride in the middle of the night and a passing car played her favorite song. Grace's mother didn't understand such things, so the sweater was donated and the old letters recycled.

Underneath Danny's bed, in an unassuming black box, Grace found a collection of journals. She opened the one on top. The writer had left hard traces on each page, evidence of the way she held her pen, the weight of her hand, her preference for dark ink. Each page was titled with a place and its address. Some of the notes were practical—*coffee is shit, AC never works, owned by racists, guacamole is overpriced.* Others were elusive references to structures without ceilings, wailing sounds, blurry memories, ghost sightings. The cold traveled from Grace's fingertips through the tops of her hands, up her arms, and landed on her lips.

She picked through the red lipsticks at a Walgreens beauty aisle around the corner from the house: *Russian Red, Cherry Bomb, Hot*

Passion, Candy Apple, Diva, Cruella Velvet, Red Velvet, Pure Red,
Blood Red, Red Hot, Hot Red, Red Passion, Candy Russian, Blood
Blood Blood, Sunday Bloody Sunday, Just Like Your Mama Used to
Make Red, Blood Bomb, Mulan Rouge, Crimson. Despite her dili-
gent note-taking, Rebecca hadn't recorded her preferred shade,
but Grace needed to know which red would look best smeared
on her own lips and around her mouth. Which would be best
to draw outside the lines of her lips. Instead, she drew thick,
hot, candy-cruel, velvety, blood-red lines on her hands. No one
noticed when she slipped three tubes of *Mulan Rouge* into her
back pocket and walked over to the cash register to pay for bottles of water and sunscreen. Max was waiting outside, in his car.
As Grace exited the store, an older woman and man walked in.
"Look at that pretty little Chinese girl," the woman said to her
companion. "Do you see her?" Grace looked over at Max; his
windows were down, so he should have been able to hear the
woman's comment. But he didn't look up from his phone, and
she had no one to roll her eyes at.

They were on their way to a beach that Max promised would
blow her away. "You've never seen a beach like this," he said.
Grace fought off the urge to laugh; while her childhood friends
often packed themselves into parents' cars to reach the water
by any means necessary, Grace had always preferred to stay on
land. But when they arrived at the beach and Grace took it in, its
sandy surface covered with smooth bleached oak tree bones, she
gasped. She ran her hand over the trunks, ducked underneath a
jungle gym of branches.

"What do you think?" Max asked. He smiled at her obvious
awe, clearly proud of himself.

"It's beautiful," Grace whispered.

The day was overcast, but still so hot that Grace felt melted. They set down their things and Grace sprinted for the water, Max not too far behind her. Despite her previous aversion, Grace rushed into the waves, ducking underneath to fully submerge her body. She knew Max was close, felt him before he wrapped his arms around her playfully. He kissed her shoulder. "You taste salty," he said. Grace turned from the waves and faced the shore. It was empty, only their two beach chairs, and cooler among the trees. She let the waves push into her back, moving her body forward without ever toppling her down. Max swam like a small child in the white foam, occasionally approaching her, grabbing her thighs or her hands or her waist. He giggled and she smiled, imagining how blissfully happy he must feel to be with a girl who flew thousands of miles to be with him on this beautiful, dead beach.

When the tips of her fingers were sufficiently pruned, Grace walked back to her beach chair, sat down, and dug her feet into the sand. Max followed her and plopped himself into his own chair. He picked up his phone and started gliding his finger over the screen. Grace tilted her head back and let the sun hit her face, and her tired body rest.

When Max first proposed she fly out to see him, Grace had played it off as a joke. "I don't even know you."

"What do you mean? We talk on the phone every night." She conceded with silence. "I think this could be something special. I don't want to regret not doing something because it scared me. Do you?"

That's where he was wrong. Grace wasn't scared to meet him. Max was easy. He was kind and good-looking. She wasn't putting herself in any real danger with him.

"Gracie?" Nobody called her that. It was a nickname that was meant to pull at her heartstrings, but it only made her nauseous.

"I'll think about it," she said.

She texted him the next morning and agreed to the trip. She had her tickets booked thirty minutes later. If someone had asked her why she'd changed her mind so quickly, why she'd been so impulsive, Grace would have hesitated. She would have hesitated to say that she'd dreamt about Rebecca, and in her dreams, Rebecca always told her to see him, to come.

Grace awoke to Max's snores. His shirt covered his face and his bare chest was red. She stood up to explore the pools of water forming among the black rocks. She'd leave in a few days, head back to Los Angeles with a deeper emptiness in her stomach than she had arrived with. Rebecca was everywhere, but Grace wasn't satisfied. She rushed toward the water again, wanting to feel enveloped by its cold. She swam out until Max was a blur, a dot blending into the white sand. He was standing now, waving his arms above his head. And what would he do if she stopped treading, stopped moving her legs? What would he do if she drowned?

What would she do?

The Devil's School was close to where the 95 and 10 converged. According to Rebecca's notes, it had been abandoned for years and now mostly stood on stories of its dead students haunting the building. Rebecca had traced the letters of its name D E V I L S S C H O O L D E V I L S S C H O O L D E V I L S S C H O O L at least three times. The text was bolded. The paper was torn. The ink had bled through to the next page.

Nature had reclaimed the school long ago. Weeds had sprung up through the concrete floor, crept up the brick walls, and covered over the graffiti. A Popeyes chicken container stood motionless on what had once been a window ledge, but everything else inside the school felt like it was moving—rustling. Empty spaces feel more alive, Grace thought; in the quiet, you can hear them sigh.

Grace sat down on the stage of the former auditorium. Its roof was torn off like the tin top of a sardine can, and the sky shone through to the grass-covered floor. In her notebook, Rebecca wrote about a cannibalistic principal who called students into his office who never came back out; she asked about eating human flesh, *What do you think it tastes like? Do you think it tastes like dog?* Grace's laugh echoed and filled the space. She imagined passing children quickening their pace to tell their friends that two women were laughing inside the Devil's School, that the ghosts had come back, that they sounded hungry.

She imagined Rebecca was there, sitting next to her, the sunlight playing with her skin until she shone, golden. Grace linked her arm with Rebecca's and laid her head on her shoulder. Rebecca leaned over and kissed her on the forehead. *What do you think it tastes like? Do you think it tastes like dog?* They laughed together.

"A guy asked me how I taste today," Grace told her. Rebecca rolled her eyes but squeezed her hand. She nuzzled into her ear and whispered, "You taste good." She kissed her neck, grabbed the hem of her shorts. They giggled again.

"What was it like, coming out to your parents?" Rebecca asked Grace. She played with Grace's hair, twisted its strands between her fingers.

"I told my mom I liked girls when I was fourteen," Grace said. "But all she did was shake her head. She told me to stop talking about it." They wrapped their arms around each other. Rebecca kissed Grace's mouth, gently prodded Grace's tongue with her own.

"She told me to come back when I was twenty-five and tell her again," Grace said after their lips parted.

"So you told her at midnight on your twenty-fifth birthday?" Rebecca asked.

"No," Grace said. "I couldn't."

Two women laughed inside the Devil's School. The ghosts came back. They tasted like dog.

He took her to a nice restaurant—the kind with white tablecloths and low lighting.

"Well hey there!" said the waitress, interrupting Grace's thoughts. "I haven't seen y'all in a really long time. Like over a year." Max didn't say anything to correct her. He just smiled and nodded.

"Sorry," he said after the waitress took their drink orders. "I think people are just used to seeing me with Rebecca."

"We don't look alike," Grace said.

"Of course you don't," he said. "You're completely different." He reached over to grab her hand. *Does he wonder what I taste like?*

"It's weird that it has to be said, though," she told him. She retracted her hand.

"Are you mad at me?" he asked. He looked like a three-legged puppy asking to hop up onto the couch. *What if we taste the same?*

"No," she said. This time she grabbed his hand. "I'm just getting used to being with you in person."

"It's weird," he said. *I wonder what she tasted like.* "But good weird?"

She smiled, without showing her teeth. "Good weird."

"I like your lipstick," he told her.

"Do you only date white guys?" Danny asked her the next morning. They had enlisted Grace to chop onions and peppers for breakfast.

"Excuse me?"

Danny shrugged. "I'm just curious," they said. "Rebecca dated a lot of white guys."

"Did you ask her why?" Grace asked.

"She told me to fuck off."

"I've only dated white guys," Grace confirmed. Danny didn't press, but pushed another onion toward Grace's cutting board. "You never dated?"

"White guys?" Danny laughed, a hearty chuckle.

"No. Rebecca." Danny dropped bacon in a pan, and its sizzle filled the silence. Their backs were turned to each other, but the room was so small their bodies almost touched anyhow. "You never dated Rebecca?" Grace asked again. Her eyes burned as she cut the onion open; she wiped tears away with her wrist.

"No, we never dated," they said. They put a thick slab of butter in another pan—the room was warm and the food smelled good. Rebecca and Danny would cook together on weekend mornings, when Max had to work; Danny would crack eggs into the center of buttery toast and Rebecca would fry up potatoes. They'd sit on the porch and drink orange juice. "Never," they said again. They cooked breakfast with her every week. They saw movies together and went on long walks and knew more about each other than anyone else. They never dated. "But we were constant."

"Why did you move in here after she died?" Grace asked.

"Max didn't want to live in the house alone," they said.

"He could have found someone else. He could have moved."

Max had asked Danny to come and help him go through Rebecca's stuff, and Danny had never left. She spilled out of their cramped closet, from underneath their bed. Rebecca hadn't thrown anything away, and neither could Danny.

"I like when she's everywhere," they said.

The AC was still broken, and all the windows in the house were open. Grace was stuffed full and sleepy. She excused herself to Max's room and dropped herself down into the tangled bed sheets. She'd let Max touch her in the dark, but their real-life sex hadn't lived up to their virtual encounters. "I'm not ready," she had told him, and he was patient.

Grace pulled off her shirt and underwear, her whole body slick with sweat, her whole body wet. It was like the humidity was a person on top of her, pressing down. She turned onto her stomach and pushed a pillow between her legs. Her hips pressed forward and back. She moaned. Grace didn't dare open her eyes as she reached between her legs and felt sweat and cum. *What do you taste like?* She touched her fingers to her lips. *What do you taste like?* She licked. *What do you taste like?* Someone else's moan broke into the room. Grace kept her eyes shut. *You taste good.*

Max's white top sheet had fallen to the floor. When Grace caught her breath, she sat up and moved off the bed. She wrapped the fallen sheet around her body and walked out of the room, toward the shower.

The faint sound of falling water could be heard in the bedroom. The fitted sheet had come undone from the left corner of the bed. One pillow sat at the head, the other in the middle.

Around it, you could see the impression of a body, a wet body, legs wrapped tightly around it. And if you looked closer, another impression—another body—could be seen, wrapped around the first.

One-Thousand-Year-Old Ghosts

Popo taught me to pickle memories when I was thirteen. It's just like cucumbers, radishes, cabbage. I learned to cut them into even squares. Memories cut like apples; the knife slides through their protective skin with a crisp snap. I packed them in jars filled with salt, sugar, vinegar, and water. No herbs and spices because they can distort the memories, make them seem too sweet or too bitter.

"It's a family secret," she said to me. "It allows you to forget."

"Forget what?" I asked.

"Anything. Forgetting does not come easily to the women in our family. We have our jars."

"What are we trying to forget, Popo?"

"So many questions. Chop this into smaller pieces."

We started with minor moments: (1) When I dropped my underwear on the floor of the changing room after swim practice at school and Abigail Kincaid picked it up and showed the whole class. (2) The time I tugged on a strange woman's skirt in a Costco checkout line because I thought, for a second, that she was my mother. (3) A recurring nightmare of being alone in an abandoned building, no way to get out.

"How do you feel?" Popo asked, after the first lids were tightened.

It felt like clenching and unclenching my jaw. Like a steady beat of tension and release. It felt like being full and empty at the same time. Instead of telling her this, I only shrugged.

She never asks him about a future where he does not come back. When she is alone, she prays that he will return to her. She asks him what he would like for dinner. Before they go to bed, she prays business will stay good. Their silence is steady; it endures. It is a silence they have agreed to.

He travels back and forth between their apartment in San Francisco and southern China. It is rare to have a husband whose body tastes like the Pacific Ocean. It is rare to have a husband made mostly of salt.

I was Popo's daughter's daughter, but our saltwater bond was stronger than blood. We exhausted my mother.

"Ma, why are you teaching her that?" she asked. It was a gray Sunday morning, and Popo was helping me pickle a few things. It had been a bad week.

"Because you won't," Popo said.

"Do you have your own jars, Mom?" I asked. I'd already searched for them, without any luck.

"No," she said. Like Popo, my mother was good at shutting down conversations. There were many times she felt far away. My arms never quite reached her.

"That's not true, Anne," Popo said. "We made you one or two when you were younger. You remember."

"Is that right?" Mom wasn't looking at either of us. She was holding a paper napkin she had used at breakfast, trying to smooth out the creases with her fingers.

"Yes," Popo said.

"I'm sick of this." My mother's fingers shredded the napkin to pieces. "How come you decide what all of us remember or forget?" There was water in her eyes. I wanted to wipe it away for her, but I was afraid her tears would not be like mine. I was afraid my mother was not made of salt.

"You know what, Ma?" my mother said. "I remember everything."

The street outside their apartment is loud the way city streets often are. The sound drifts in through the open windows of the front room, and she lets it fill the space he left behind. It sits in his favorite chair, the blue one next to the fireplace. After it is well rested, it moves across the room and embeds itself into the cracks in the floorboards. It touches all of his books, then settles into his side of the bed. She holds it as she falls asleep. She smells it in her hair the next morning. She keeps it there until the rest of the city wakes up and it makes its way outside again.

When he comes home, he shuts the windows, says he is tired of loud noises. He tells her how the ocean roars and the wind cracks. He tells her he has been looking forward to the silence of home.

My mother went through my room to find my jars. She displayed the five she'd found tucked into my sock drawer. Both my mother and my jars confronted me when I got home from school.

"I know Popo thinks this is best, but memories are important even when they are painful. I'm concerned about you," she said. "Both of you."

"I'm fine, Mom. Popo is fine," I said.

"She's not fine. Her short-term memory is getting worse. She forgets where she puts things, she doesn't show up to appointments, she can't even tell me what she had for breakfast some days. Popo isn't fine." Her voice was clear and calm, but the sound of it bounced around inside my head until it ached.

I looked at my jars, lined up on the kitchen counter, and tried to remember what was in them. They could have been anyone's jars. The liquid inside was murky. I wanted to open them. I wanted to push them off the ledge, to see them break open as they hit the floor.

"Do you really remember everything?" I asked her. I tried to remember stories about her before she had me, ones that she must have told me, but I couldn't find any.

"Nobody remembers everything," she said.

"But you told Popo—"

"I was upset."

"Tell me what you remember."

We stayed at the kitchen table, and she talked. The darkness slipped into the room and sat down with us. I couldn't see my mother's gaze through the dark—we hadn't turned the lights on—but I could feel it on my skin.

Things she told me: Popo would prepare for Gung Gung's homecomings with his favorite dishes—winter melon soup and salted duck. Popo would wear a pink dress on those days because she said Gung Gung was tired of the blues and greens of the ocean. Popo's comforter was white and felt like velvet, even though it was only made of cotton. Popo would let my mother sleep with her when Gung Gung was away. My mother met my father when they both worked for an insurance company in downtown Sacramento. They were both already married, but my father asked my mother out for a drink one day after work and she said yes. Popo liked my father because he was really American, unlike my mother's first husband, who grew up in Chinatown, like her. My parents loved each other so much that she was never hungry. When my father left without saying goodbye, my mother ate everything in the refrigerator and the pantry and the cupboards.

The memories came in pieces. Sometimes she stumbled, searched for more to tell me. She wanted to fill the silence but didn't have enough words. When she was done, she asked me how I felt, and I didn't have the heart to tell her that it felt the same. It felt like clenching and unclenching my jaw, that steady beat of tension and release. Full and empty, at the same time.

She is less lonely now that she has Anne. She has something to hold on to when she walks through Chinatown, something to ground her to the sidewalk. She used to think that she would float away. Now she walks with purpose.

She teaches Anne how to say "apple" and "block" in English. She does not talk to her in Cantonese. When she doesn't know the word she is looking for in English, she says nothing.

As I got older, I filled my jars, and it was a feeling larger than relief. I poured out jams, mayonnaise, and peanut butter. I clogged every drain in the house to create space to put myself away.

(1) The song that was playing when I lost my virginity to a boy who changed the sheets right after. (2) The white woman at the grocery store who told me I was prettier because I wasn't "full Chinese." Her hands in my hair: "You're so lucky," she said. (3) The men who leered at me when I walked down the street, and the one who told me, "I've never had one like you before."

(4) How my mother looked after the spindled cancer cells settled into her body. (5) The woman on the bus who spoke to me in Cantonese, and how I didn't know how to respond. How I searched for the words that someone should've taught me, but I couldn't find them anywhere.

Popo never warned me not to let it become a habit, a practice, a daily ritual. Mom wasn't around to count my jars, display them, remind me of what I had forgotten, witness my slow dissolve. I made the pickling liquid in large batches. I bought sugar and vinegar in bulk. My jars overflowed and spilled onto my hands until they stung.

Every time he comes back, he feels more foreign. He says, "Néih hóu ma," but she responds in English. She practices with Anne. She learns new words every day.

"One day Anne's children will not know how to speak our language," he tells her.

She wants to say, "Maybe that will be for the best. They'll stop longing for things they cannot have. There will be no reason to leave. Not everyone can live in between. Not everyone can survive being split into two. There are fish that die in saltwater."

Popo drank a glass of saltwater every night before her evening prayers. One night, I asked her why. She said it was a leftover habit from when my Gung Gung would travel. "He died on his way back to China. Did you know that?"

"You told me," I said.

"I just wanted to make sure you didn't forget."

She mixed table salt with water from the kitchen sink. She took her time, drank it while she was reading a magazine. I never requested a glass, and she never offered.

"Popo?" I asked, after her glass was washed and set down to dry. "What do you put in your jars?"

"I don't remember," she said. "That is their purpose."

"But aren't there things you wish you hadn't forgotten?" I asked.

She looked at me for a long time before she answered no. Then she added in a softer voice, "Sometimes I think there are not enough jars in this city."

He is dying but refuses to die in America. "I am going home," he says. "I cannot be buried here." He makes the necessary travel arrangements. He plans to leave in only a few weeks.

"You are leaving me here," she says to him.

"Yes."

"What am I supposed to do without you?" she asks. "What about Anne?"

"What does it matter? I am dying either way." He looks at her and smiles. "You don't want my ghost to haunt you. It's better for both of us if I go."

"Yes," she says. "You're right."

To guarantee that she is not haunted by her dead husband, she stuffs most of what she has of him into thirty-seven glass jars. She only leaves enough to tell her future grandchildren (1) his name, (2) his occupation, (3) where he was born, (4) where he died, and (5) the saltiness of his breath.

She does not have a yard to bury the jars, so instead she pushes him underneath her bed. The first night she sleeps with them, she hears a steady humming. It keeps her awake. It never goes away, but she never moves the jars. She learns to live with the hum until she forgets it is there at all.

"Anne, grab the measuring cups," she said one afternoon.

"Popo," I said. "I'm Katie. Anne was my mother."

Her eyebrows furrowed. She moved around me and grabbed the measuring cups herself.

"Please stop. This is making you sick," I said.

She continued to measure and chop. She licked her index finger, dipped it into a bowl of salt in front of her, and popped it back in her mouth to taste.

I wanted to imitate her, feel the small grains on my own tongue, but I stopped myself.

"I'm close," she said.

"Close to what? What else could you have to forget?" I slammed my hands on the counter. Her bowl of salt shook.

We stood in silence until she said, "I love you, but I wish I remembered how to say it the other way."

"What do you mean?" I asked.

The tears on her face looked milky white.

"There was a way I used to say it. I don't remember the words. I used to say it to someone," she said. "Do you remember?"

"No, Popo," I said. "I don't."

When she takes care of Katie, she does not put her down. Katie's skin is soft underneath her fingertips, and she wonders how much sadness this little body can take. She smells just like Anne did when she was a baby but looks so different. There are only traces of Anne in the baby's face, and it makes Katie harder to hold on to. She is half-ghost. If she puts Katie down, she will disappear. She will not be able to find her again. She holds on to her because this is not a thing she can let go of.

By the end, her pickling process had picked up speed. Everything I loved about her became smaller and smaller until she started to break apart in my hands, to fall through my permanently wrinkled fingertips. Seven years after my mom died, Popo finished dissolving.

My memory was shaky. Most of the water in my body was salt. I no longer had difficulty forgetting; it came easily, with or without a jar. Remembering was harder.

As I packed up her home, I looked for all the places where Popo had put herself to rest. I walked through each room, sat on each chair, picked up each knickknack, ran my fingers over every book's spine. I went through all of her drawers and closets. I took every lid off every box. Jars were hidden everywhere.

She was right. There hadn't been enough jars in the city to hold everything she needed to put away. She'd started to fill milk jugs and ice cream pints. Even her shampoo bottles and toothpaste tubes had memories stuffed inside them.

I laid them out in her living room. They took up every inch of the floor. I balanced them on top of each other. They sank between couch cushions. One or two rolled behind the television. I played a childhood game to choose one: *My mother said to pick the very best one and that is—*

Like the others, its contents blurred in the murky liquid. I wanted it to look familiar, but of course it didn't. I pulled at the lid, but my hands kept slipping. I was too weak, or the jar was too strong, or whatever was inside didn't want to be taken back.

I threw it against the wall. The glass shattered, the liquid dripped to the floor, and the memory clung to the paint. Its smell surprised me—orange peels and baby powder. Popo was holding my mother's head in her lap, pushing her hair back with her hands, cooing to her softly. The memory played in a loop, but each time something was different. Sometimes, Popo's shirt was a different color; other times, my mother's head rested on her shoulder; once my mother looked older, then younger. I couldn't pick it up; it kept slipping out of my hands.

One by one, I opened the rest of the jars. Some smelled rancid, like death. Memories of her travels from China, of her first few years living in San Francisco, of my mother's sickness and her funeral. Many smelled like the ocean, like Gung Gung's seawater breath, like the smells that made up her heartbreak. The memories of me smelled like vanilla yogurt and strawberries.

The floor was wet. I lay down in the mess and let my clothes soak it all up. If my mother and Popo had been there, I would have told them this: (1) I still long for things I cannot have. (2) I am not split in two, but I am still living between things. (3) We are drowning in all this saltwater.

Real Bodies

You don't know what you look like. Sometimes when you're at your desk at work, your fingers start to twitch and your knees shake. Sweat accumulates at your temples and your lip starts to bleed because you've been biting it. You get the overwhelming urge to go to the bathroom to make sure you're still there, to remind yourself of where your eyes sit on your face and how brown your skin is. When you're out on dates and men tell you that you're beautiful, you smile and nod the way you're supposed to. You want to ask them what they see when they look at you. You want them to describe how your eyes sit on your face and how brown your skin is. You want them to point to another woman in the restaurant and say, "Her. You look like her and she looks like you." You need a point of comparison, a second opinion.

When you cannot find your reflection, you resort to touch. You feel for your left arm with your right fingers, all five of them. Each one drags across the bumps on your skin. Once you have confirmed that your left arm is there and your right fingers are touching it, you lose one of your earlobes or your whole neck.

Your body is constantly looking for itself, remembering itself. It's nothing like people who lose their limbs, but you still think of your lost body parts as ghostly, weightless, always at risk of floating away from you forever.

You log in to your account every morning to prove that you're trying. Some say it's a rumor that you're monitored, that your chats are reviewed, your movement tracked before and after The Website™. It's only a rumor, but you rehearse every click and keystroke. You tap a button on the top right of your computer screen with your right thumb. The webcam's red light turns on and scans your retinas. You check your inbox—no new matches. The red and pink envelope is empty. Even on a government-run website, a candy-heart veneer is embedded into the code. A frowning cupid mocks you as it flies around the window.

This is not a website where you initiate conversations, complete personality tests, or rank people by their pictures and whether they like flan. You remember a time when you would ignore the men who wanted to know where you were from. The ones who wanted to run their hands through your thick dark hair, wanted to know what your mother cooks for you when you're sad. Responses are required now. They're watching you. You could get into some deep shit. There's no space to share that you like flan because you've always imagined your Popo liked flan even though your mom says that isn't true.

On The Website™, your matches are selected by the state. You think there was a time, maybe a few years ago, when all websites were going to be turned over to the federal government, but it didn't happen. It makes more sense this way—what's the point if a woman in Wisconsin is paired with a man in New Mexico? Long-distance relationships are not the point. They are hard to control. Despite science's best efforts, you cannot procreate over the internet yet.

It's framed like a choice, like you can pick from a multitude of people who are carefully selected just for you, but there are guidelines. There are expectations. There are rules. You click a box and agree.

- ☐ There are only two sexes, male and female, determined at birth. Men are paired with women. Women are paired with men.
- ☐ You belong to a specific class: A, B, C, D, E, or F. Your class corresponds to how much money you have in the bank, your race, where you grew up, where you went to school, how much money your parents have in the bank, your job, etc. You are only matched with people in your class or the ones directly below and above it. This is to create a sense of mobility.
- ☐ White people can match with other white people, but people of color can only match with white people. This is to create a sense of mobility.
- ☐ You are not who you think you are. You do not want what you think you want.

Carol picks you up and drives you to work. She works with you at the university. You drive with Carol because she knows all the words to pop songs on the radio. You like to watch her bob her head in time to the music. Sometimes you're afraid that she is going to crash the car because she closes her eyes during the best parts. It's worth it because you like to watch her and she doesn't mind when you do.

She honks her horn when she's outside instead of sending you a text. There are rumors that they can read your text messages.

Carol stopped using her cell phone a few weeks ago. She drops by without calling and shoves handwritten notes underneath doors instead of sending emails.

"Any new prospects?" she asks. Even Carol can't avoid The Website™. If she didn't log in, somebody would contact her. They would email her, text her, call her. Someone would knock down her door and force her to look at pictures and profiles until she said yes to one.

"No, thank God. Last night was awful," you tell her.

"Tell me about it," Carol says. "I have two tonight—Luke and Matthew."

"Together?"

"I wish! No, I'm trying a double feature tonight—a two-birds-one-stone type thing." She asks you to hold the wheel so she can pull her mass of curls into a bun on top of her head.

She has a white mom and Black dad, and you have a Chinese mom and a white dad. Both of your parents married only a short time after it was legal to do so. Now, you and Carol are held up as examples. Beauty is just enough white to soften the rough edges.

"It's exhausting," she says. "Do you remember it always being this exhausting?"

"Like before?" you ask. She nods. She is holding a hairpin between her lips. "I barely remember before."

"Back then, you could stare across the room at someone and think about what'd it be like to fool around with them in the back seat of a car." She sighs, and you wish you could breathe in all the air her body pushes out, sit on her lap, and inhale as she exhales.

You shrug. "That was forever ago."

Your parents were married to other people before they married each other. They both had other children, one son each. You have two half-brothers—one white, one Chinese—and you fit snugly between them. When you are out with your family, you are often reminded that you are the piece that makes it work. You are the thing that allows it to make sense. Your brothers, Brad and Lawrence, are both married. They found their matches on The Website™ a few years ago and settled into middle-class suburbia. They are having children now. Their broods will look just like you.

The hot air outside sticks to your skin; heat swells and fills up the almost-empty campus. You open the only window in your office and leave the lights off. There is something in your shoe. It's small, but you can't ignore it. Your foot is aching. When it becomes too much, you push your shoe off by its heel. Relief floods you—it rushes up from your foot, through your body, all the way to your shoulders. The phone rings.

"Hello?" you answer.

"Hello Ms. [redacted], this is [redacted] calling from The Website™!" The voice is cheery and you imagine its owner dressed like a cherub. You almost hang up the phone, but you know it wouldn't do any good. They know where you are.

"How can I help you?" you say in a voice like syrup. You hope [redacted] thinks you suck on candy hearts all day—maybe one that says BE MINE.

"I was just looking through your account records and I saw that you do not have any matches for today," the voice says. You think the voice wants a response, but it doesn't. "That's a mistake. I'm making arrangements for you to meet a man named Barry. He is an accountant from Class C. His listed interests include water skiing and Jay-Z. I will send you an email regarding when and where you are to meet him, along with a picture."

"We don't live near a body of water," you say.

"I'm sorry?"

"You said he likes to water ski, but we don't live near a body of water."

"Yes, well—" the cheeriness drains out of the voice, annoyance settling into its chords. This voice is not meant for conversation; it's meant to dispense information. It pauses for only a moment. "Check your email."

Click.

Barry looks like a ghost. He is smiling in the picture, and it sends a chill through your body. There is a link embedded in the email takes you to Barry's profile. You confirm that he does indeed like water skiing and Jay-Z. The Website™ has determined that you are 98 percent compatible, a true love match. You imagine the ghost children you would have with him. You picture their light brown hair and white skin. You wonder if you could ever love a ghost child. How would you hug them without your hands going straight through their small ghost bodies?

After work, you asked Carol if you could come over—you didn't want to go home alone—and she said yes. It's not encouraged, women being alone together. They have become skeptical of friendship. They remember the intimacy of such relationships. Sleepovers past the age of puberty are not encouraged. Multi-stall bathrooms with large mirrors have been converted into single-stall rooms. There is a curfew for women without male escorts. There are hotlines for neighbors to call if they notice a friend staying over too late.

You scrunch Carol's sheets until your palms sweat and your fingers ache. You want the pull of gravity to be stronger so you can sink deeper into the mattress. When her back is turned, you put your head down on her pillow. You imagine what her sweat would smell like if it mixed with yours. Her shampoo smells like almonds and sweet milk. You want to wash your hair.

"What about this?" She's holding a striped dress to her body. She wore it once to work and then to an office holiday party. You remember how the sleeves rested on her wrists and how you wanted to kiss them. You've never wanted to kiss someone's wrist before.

"I don't know. What about the black one instead?" you say. You want to kiss her wrists less when she wears the black dress. She nods her head.

You try to remember what this looked like before The Website™. You would ask to kiss her and she would nod. You'd cup the back of her head, and your fingers would get tangled in her hair. The kiss would be soft until it wasn't anymore. There would be urgency, but it'd be born out of desire, not fear.

She drags lipstick over her mouth until it turns red. She's ready. She gets a notification on her laptop, a cheery ping. Her date is on his way. You tell her she looks beautiful. You are close enough to feel the heat coming off her body, close enough that you feel everything that makes up you and her. You think that you could live off this feeling forever. Even if you could never touch her, you could stand close enough to feel these vibrations, and it would be enough.

Barry looks at you the way people always look at you. He brings you to a nice place. The white candlesticks melt down to the white tablecloth until the wax disappears into the fabric. The plates are white. You're so focused on the table settings that you can't recall what the rest of the room looks like. You're afraid to look up, afraid to see the other women there on dates. Afraid you'll see yourself—or, worse, Carol—reflected in their performances.

"Where are you from?" he asks. You tell him where. He looks confused. The Website™ doesn't publicize information on ethnicity. Their official policy is that "labels divide us." They say that it won't matter in the future, anyway.

"My mom is Chinese and my dad is white." He's relieved.

"You know, my parents aren't too thrilled about this whole thing," he says. "You know, the direction The Website™ is taking us. I think they hoped I'd settle down with a girl from my church." You nod your head and smile, like you are supposed to. "But I think they'd really like you. You're beautiful, and just different enough. Our children might get lucky and have blue eyes. Think how pretty their skin would be. Such a light caramel color." He's getting excited now, talking about suburbs you could move to and how advanced your kids would be. He stuffs meat and potatoes in his mouth. This is your American dream.

You take him home with you because it's not against the rules when he's a white man. You want to know what it feels like. You want confirmation. He asks you where your bedroom is and then he leads you there. He pushes you down onto the bed and smiles. He bites your skin hard enough to bruise it. You feel the vessels breaking, leaking out. He puts his body inside your body, first his tongue, then his fingers, then his dick. He asks if this is how you like it and you wonder if maybe it is. He lifts you off the bed and into the air; you lose contact with your newly stained sheets. You hear yourself echoing him. *I like it. I like it. I like it.* When it's over, his whole body surrounds you in an embrace. He squeezes you tight and it feels like he's keeping you together. He tells you that you are beautiful and you wonder what that means about your eyes and your skin and your parents and your children and your children's children. You do not smile. You pretend to sleep.

You're standing on top of your apartment building. It's only five flights up, but you can see the city stretched out before you. Mrs. Costello, your downstairs neighbor, is parking her car in the lot behind the building. You almost wave to her, but then think better of it. Mrs. Costello doesn't like you very much. She, like many of her generation, is wary of you and yours. She thinks you're a sweet girl but doesn't understand this online dating business. It's just not right. Besides, she probably doesn't even see you.

Large ceramic planters surround the building, and you wonder if one would catch you if you jumped. You imagine the sky pushing and the earth pulling you down, and your bones start to tingle inside of your skin. You step onto the ledge because you want to feel the force of gravity, the impact of cement, ceramic, and dirt. You think you'll find your body whole if you can, just this once, sink deeper into the earth.

Suwannee

FRIDAY

The river water looked tea-soaked as it met the colder, clearer water coming from the natural spring. Danny moved against the river's current, their arms spread out in an attempt to balance. They had fallen early in the afternoon, a bruise already coming to the surface of their skin. One of their hands was holding a contraband beer can, the label covered by a coozie from a local brewery.

"Where are you going?" Lou called out to them. Danny shrugged. Their belongings were spread among the cypress knees on a thin strip of muddy shore set against a steep drop-off. Towels, two coolers, backpacks, and discarded shorts and T-shirts marked their territory.

Rachel, Melissa, and Taylor sat on a yellow blanket, their exposed bellies shielded by the trees, while Danny moved closer to the sun-touched water upstream. They wanted to feel the sun on their skin, the multiple summer shades of brown on their body. Lou and a few others floated on flamingo-, unicorn-, and doughnut-shaped inner tubes. Scattered among a dozen or so

vacationing families, their brightly colored group of seven cel-
ebrated Danny's birthday. Despite only being a two-hour drive
from Jacksonville, they had found an affordable house to rent
and squeezed themselves between other people's family photos
and childhood toys.

No one noticed Rebecca, her lithe body slithering through the
Suwannee like a snake. Danny's back faced her as she reached
her hand toward their thigh and tickled it gently with her nails.

"What—" Danny's surprise was enveloped by Rebecca's gig-
gles. "Jesus! Rebecca!" She jumped on their back, her arms around
their neck and legs locked around their belly. Their soft body
supported her weight easily in the water. She rested her head on
their back in a sort-of apology. Her long, wet black hair stuck to
their skin and draped over their shoulder, covering their chest.

"Your boobs are going to pop out," she warned them. She gently pulled the top of their swimsuit to cover up their large chest.

"I know," they said. "This bathing suit barely keeps them in. I
can't wait to get rid of them."

"Soon," she assured them.

Rebecca got off their back, lying down once again in the water.
She held on to two rocks so the river wouldn't sweep her away.

"I love you, Dan," she told them in a singsong voice.

Watching her wiggle like an eel in the water, their heart
burst with tenderness for their friend. A few years before they
wouldn't have known what to do with that affection, a love so
sticky and easy and warm.

"I love you too, Becky," they told her.

Her face contorted in protest. "I hate when you call me that."

The water was deep and clear, and Ashley looked like a mermaid from where Danny stood at the top of the wooden stairs

leading into the natural pool. Her long legs and arms moved her through the water around mamas holding younger children with inflatable floaties around their arms and groups of splashing teenagers. If she hadn't worn a flashy green and orange bathing suit, they might have lost her as she dove into the deeper shadows of the cavernous spring. Danny launched into the pool with an almost graceful dive and felt the water shock their system. Beneath the surface, the rock formations looked prehistoric. When Danny and Ashley resurfaced, they both noticed how the water looked like glitter in her natural hair.

"How's your birthday so far?" she asked them.

"Perfect," they told her. Their arms moved through the water slowly, their legs doing the heavy lifting in keeping their bodies afloat. Neither could see the bottom.

"I like that there are so many Black and brown families here," Ashley said. She turned to face the entrance to the river, where a group of Black kids played on a small strip of sand, their mamas and aunties laughing in lounge chairs only a few feet away. "You don't always see that when you go the springs."

"The Confederate flags don't help," Danny responded. They were reminded of the Florida state song, *Way Down upon the Swanee River / Far, far away*, a minstrel song written by a man who had never even seen the Suwannee. They felt the weight of it in their chest, wanted to expand their brown, queer body so that everyone there had to see it. They were overwhelmed by it—by Florida, by its warmth and its beauty and everything that lurked beneath.

Ashley nodded her head, and Danny wanted to know more about what she thought. Her intense quiet had always pulled them in. She had the tendency to look at them, to look at everyone, hard and serious, never giving away what she saw.

"How are you feeling? With Melissa and Lou," Danny asked her. Ashley and Melissa had recently broken up after nearly a year of dating. It was, like so many queer breakups, a quiet explosion, and now Lou and Melissa were sneaking off into the woods together, holding hands when they thought no one was looking.

"It's fine," Ashley said quickly. "I'm fine." She looked over her shoulder as if expecting them to be there, blissed out in their own kind of sunshine.

It wasn't easy, holding so many feelings in your hands when the place they lived was already small and hostile. It was better to keep each other close, to try not to dispose of one another, even if doing so ravaged your lonely and sad heart.

Danny didn't want to make things more complicated, but they also wanted to slide their hand closer to Ashley's, to touch her pinky finger with theirs, to lean in and kiss her shoulder. They didn't move their hand, and their whole arm ached with the effort to keep still.

"You know, it's not so bad," Ashley said, interrupting their silence. "The more I think about it, the more it makes sense. Me and Melissa weren't meant to be."

"That's good," Danny said. "I wasn't sure if you'd come when you found out they were both coming, but I'm really glad you did."

"Me too," she said.

Their knees touched hers and their skin broke out in goose bumps. They wondered if she noticed, if she assumed it was because of the cold water.

Rebecca had put herself in charge of the sleeping arrangements, her own refusal to let awkwardness and heartache ruin Danny's birthday trip. Ashley would room with her and Danny, upstairs, far away from Lou and Melissa. She often took charge of things that no one asked her to take charge of, and it usually worked out for the better when she did.

"I'm not going to pretend nothing's happening. We all know they want to sleep together. I might as well give them a room together," Rebecca said. She didn't have time to pretend she didn't know what she knew. "Anyhow, do they really believe that sneaking around is somehow sparing Ashley's feelings?"

Danny started to answer, but Rebecca didn't stop to take a breath.

"Because she knows. We all know," she said.

"Well, I—" Danny started.

"No, I can't even talk about it, Danny. I'm too annoyed."

"Okay."

Danny and Rebecca often shared rooms together, beds together, couches together. They were used to waking up to her arms wrapped around their belly, and her face smushed into their chest. Danny knew that she liked to sleep with a pillow between her legs, that at least one of her feet would always escape the confines of the quilt and comforter. Despite this and the Florida heat, she always had two blankets on top of her, needing to feel the weight atop her body, to feel pressed down into the mattress.

They drank fire whiskey around the fire even though the night air was warm. They'd made a large dinner, and most of the group was starting to feel sleepy from alcohol and food. Nobody would go to bed early that night, though. They would push past their tiredness and remain around the fire, and then the kitchen table, until the sky lightened again.

"Cheers, to Danny!" Lou said, lifting their glass.

"To Danny," their friends shouted alongside the sounds of clinking glass.

"Happy birthday, baby!" Rebecca squealed. "We love you." She leaned over and kissed their cheek. Danny blushed.

Danny caught Ashley's eyes across the fire and smiled at her. She smiled back and winked. They held each other's gaze for what felt like a long time, until Ashley saw Melissa and Lou stand up and make their way toward the trails attached to the property.

"Where are you going?" Rebecca yelled after them.

"Just on a walk!" Melissa yelled back.

"It's dark," Rebecca said, loud enough for them to hear.

"We have headlamps!" Lou called to her.

Danny watched Ashley's face, waited to see what would break through as she watched them. She remained still, smiled, and then met Danny's eyes again. They gave her a shrug, and she stuck her lip out in a pout. She looked at them with a sweetness that made their chest tighten and their skin burn. It made them want to write bad poetry about her, about how she was like the moon.

"Let's play a game," Taylor said, their energy like a summer storm. They were built like a crane—a tall and reedy dancer who always seemed to be going into or just coming out of an arabesque.

"What are we playing?" Ashley asked.

"Mafia?" Rebecca asked Taylor.

"Salad bowl?" Taylor responded.

"What about that Ouija board Lou and I found in the kids' bedroom?" Rachel countered.

"Where's Lou?" Taylor asked, and Rebecca shot them a glance.

"Is that a game?" Danny asked.

"Sure it is," Rebecca said. "What else would it be?"

"I don't know." Danny shrugged. "Not sure if it's smart to fuck with spirits for fun."

Rebecca rolled her eyes and gently shoved them. "Don't be a downer. What's the worst that could happen?"

"It's Danny's birthday," Ashley interjected. "Let's do what they want to do."

All eyes turned to Danny. Around the fire, their friends looked like queer demons; the plot of *Lord of the Flies* flashed through their brain. "I feel too drunk for a game," they admitted. "What about ghost stories?"

Oooooh, they all whispered, their voices hushed by the suggestion.

Taylor went first, told them a story about a girl who turned into a lizard—scales, split tongue, the works, they said. It was less scary, more erotic. They wiggled their body like a serpent as they unraveled a story about poisoned kisses and bellies warming under heat lamps. *And now, when you go outside in the dead of summer, the rustle in the grass, the hissing in the air—that's just our lizard kin vibrating, waiting for us to join them.*

It was then that Melissa and Lou crept back to the fire, only a tad more tousled than usual. Danny watched them separate as they approached the group, settle on opposite ends of the fire with bodies to buffer either of them from Ashley. Lou sat right next to Danny, put their hand on their cheek—a brief spark on their skin.

"What'd I miss?" they asked Danny.

"Ghost stories," Danny said. "Well, sort of."

"You're being a dick," Rebecca said, suddenly between them.

"Nobody asked you."

"Well, they should," she said, and then was gone again.

"I'll tell a story," Lou said, addressing the group.

And then Rachel, and then Danny, and then Melissa went. Each telling stories about haunted houses, summer camps, under-the-bed and in-the-closet demons.

"I think it's my turn," Rebecca said gleefully. She stood over the fire, the orange glow painting her skin; she held up her hands and it was as if even the cicadas fell under her spell, were hushed, like the rest of them, in anticipation of her story.

SATURDAY

Danny climbed over Rebecca and Ashley's sleeping bodies and stumbled down the narrow steps from the attic bedroom to the kitchen, caught Lou and Melissa in a sleepy embrace.

"Morning," they said.

The couple jerked, unknotted their arms quickly.

"Morning, babe," Melissa chirped. "Do you want some coffee?"

"Please."

They sat around the unfamiliar kitchen table once they found mugs, coffee filters, sugar. Melissa poured them each a cup from the French press.

"So," Danny said. "How's it going?"

Lou sighed. Melissa shrugged.

"Why do we have to keep talking about it?" Melissa asked. "We're not doing anything wrong."

Danny lifted their hands in the air, in surrender. "I was just asking how y'all were doing. I wasn't accusing you of anything."

"It's already hard figuring out what this is"—Melissa gestured toward herself and Lou—"without the whole damn group chat chiming in."

"Fair enough," Danny said. "I don't know why you'd expect anything different, though. People are just feeling protective."

"She's the one that broke up with me," Melissa said, her voice rising in volume and pitch—whiny. Her eyes started leaking and Danny felt pangs of distrust, annoyance. They knew they should reach out to Melissa, but their arm wouldn't move to her. It took all of them not to roll their eyes at her to her face.

"Crying already?" Taylor asked as they walked into the room. They kissed the top of Melissa's head to tell her they were only joking, but her cheeks were still pink, her eyes still watery.

"Stop bullying our friends, Danny," Taylor added as they skulked around the kitchen for supplies to make breakfast. "It's not their fault they're being so messy."

"No?" Danny asked.

"Of course not! We're gay and in our twenties; it's our goddamn right."

Taylor and Danny laughed together, their big smiles matching.

"I'm over this," Lou said, and stomped their feet out of the room. The front door slammed, the screen door an echo of it.

"I guess you don't want eggs then?" Taylor yelled out after them.

Danny, Rebecca, Rachel, and Taylor had met in college, Lou and Danny as coworkers at a coffee shop they both quit a few months in. Rebecca and Ashley became friends as volunteers for a summer camp for girls and trans youth, and Melissa moved to Jacksonville after meeting Ashley in the height of lesbian Tumblr. Some of their friendships were almost eight years strong, and others were newer, but they'd all spent the past two years with their teeth sunk into each other like burrs—nights out at the bar, movies at the theater and on each other's couches, hurricane hunker-downs, and year-round barbecues. There was something about them as a group, sweet on each other in all the ways that were possible. And Danny looked for them, called to them, chose them on birthdays and holidays and celebrations and heartbreaks, like when their dad had died, and they each took turns sharing Danny's double bed with them because it was the only way they could sleep.

The disruption Melissa and Lou's recent flirtation had caused was, admittedly, annoying. It had surfaced dynamics and frustrations that before they'd all let stay underground. Suddenly it became a game of, "Is it okay if I invite ____," and new, smaller group texts sprouted. They mostly refused to acknowledge it to each other, simply adjusted to the new boundaries and tried to keep it moving while the foundation beneath them shifted.

They went to a different spring, this one more remote, one that they could claim just for themselves but for a pair of divers exploring underwater caves. In the distance, the singing of gators joined the music from their speakers.

"That sounded close," Melissa said. She froze at the edge of the spring, wrapped her arms around her body as if to protect it. These were the moments it was clear to the others that while Melissa had fit into their group seamlessly, she was still a Northern import.

"We're fine," Danny said, assuring her. They wrapped her in their arms, a silent attempt at apologizing for being hard on her at breakfast. She leaned into their body in response. They swayed together to music only they could hear, perfectly in rhythm, as if they each knew the song and the tempo. Melissa kissed Danny's arm before breaking free and diving back into the pool of water. They watched her, submerged; she pushed her arms out, flicked her legs as if they were one.

There was no river, just the clear, cold water crowded with cypress knees, hanging Spanish moss, and spiked saw palmettos. The park was named after a peacock and Danny could see it—the reflection of the blue sky, the green flora, and then the deepest blues, down below. They sat on a rock perfectly shaped and positioned so that they could still dip their feet in the water. Rebecca plopped next to them, handing them a beer fresh from the cooler. Danny shifted so their shins touched hers, popped the can open, and chugged, the cold, carbonated drink soothing their burning throat and heart simultaneously.

"How does twenty-five feel?" she asked them.

"Old."

"Already?"

"I'm tired."

"We didn't sleep that much last night," she conceded.

"Your story was too creepy," Danny said. "But please haunt me if you die."

"Promise!" Rebecca chirped, offering her pinky finger to them. The two friends tangled their fingers together and then each kissed the connecting fist.

"What's going on with you and Ashley?" she asked, eyebrow raised.

"What do you mean?"

"I don't know, just a vibe."

"What kind of vibe?"

She smiled, sipped from her soda, then crossed her eyes and let the liquid drip out of her mouth.

"You're a freak," Danny said. They laughed.

"Truly."

Taylor jumped on Lou in the water, their bodies looking like a monstrous spider as they wrestled. Melissa swam up to them, splashing and encouraging their roughhousing. Danny and Rebecca watched, clapped when Lou launched Taylor off their shoulders and Taylor found a way to dive elegantly into the water. Rebecca held up eight of her fingers, Danny held up nine.

"Tough judges," Taylor said when they broke through the surface.

Danny turned, looked for Ashley, who was perched on a towel next to Rachel, farther away from the water's edge. They each held a book in their hands but were talking instead of reading. Danny wondered what they were talking about, wanted to walk over and plop themself down next to them. Ashley used her other hand as a visor, blocking the sun. Danny watched her, couldn't stop comparing her to the celestial—last night she was the moon, now she was the sun.

Rebecca cleared her throat. "You're staring," she said.

"Am not," Danny said, but they did not turn back around.

"Stare any longer and you'll be the creepy one."

Rebecca nudged Danny's legs with her feet.

"She seems to not be bothered by Melissa and Lou, though," Rebecca prattled. "I'm glad she still came."

"Do you think it would be weird?" Danny asked. "Or that she'd even want to?"

"I think it doesn't hurt to try," Rebecca said. "I love Ashley. I love you. I think there could be something."

"You don't think it would be too messy?" They tossed a glance toward Lou and Melissa.

"I don't know, what's *too* messy?" she teased.

"We're not nineteen anymore," they said, their face settled on seriousness. Danny preferred to be a witness to their friends' relationship troubles rather than jumping into their own. They had plenty of embarrassing blunders that sometimes made it hard for them to fall asleep some nights, but nothing that made it difficult to walk into a crowded house party or bar. Instead, most of their friends and acquaintances brightened when they saw Danny, glad to see someone who hadn't drunkenly made out with their ex-girlfriend or who took a friend's side in an argument. Danny was Switzerland.

"Sure, but we're not dead either," Rebecca said with a wink. They bonked their heads together lightly, and Danny wondered at the way Rebecca, for all her hard and blunt edges, saw the absolute best in them, in most of their friends. She made Danny feel like they could get any job, move to any town, fall in love with any girl that they set their mind to. And, even if they hadn't gotten to any of those things yet, the possibility was enough.

That night, cicadas screamed into the dark sky, competing with the crack and spit of the fire. Danny could barely see a few feet in front of them as they walked around the house to the front porch. Rachel's tent and hammock were somewhere on the front lawn, but Danny couldn't remember where exactly. They found the front steps with the light of their cell phone and leaned their body against the porch railing.

It didn't take long for Ashley to appear, her flashlight and the sound of her footsteps signaling her approach.

"How's it going?" she asked.

"Oh, fine," they said. "How about you?"

"Fine."

They sat like that, looking at the stars but sensing one another. Ashley was one of the only people whose silence comforted Danny—usually, they surrounded themself with chatty people like Rebecca and Taylor who could easily fill up space with questions and jokes and laughter. Ashley laughed too, but she also liked to watch, her eyes always absorbing what happened around her. And Danny liked that about her, but sometimes wanted to know what she noticed.

"Should we talk about it?" she asked them. They shook their head, though they really meant to say, *I don't know, and what would it mean if we did?*

She sat down next to them, slipping her arm through theirs and resting her head on their shoulder. "How long have we been friends, Danny?" she asked.

"Years," they said.

She kissed their shoulder once and then twice. They turned their head toward her. Their cheeks brushed against each other and it felt like, like, like—

Don't.

Their head felt swampy, their mouth full of cotton balls absorbing all the moisture from their tongue, their throat, their teeth. They pulled back from Ashley and surprise colored her face. "Is something wrong?" she asked.

"No, no," Danny said, but they felt the bubbling of guilt, embarrassment, shame in their gut. "I'm sorry."

They couldn't look at her directly, their cheeks burned and they wondered if the heat they radiated reached her.

"I just thought—" she said, and then left it there, unfinished. And then, "But maybe you're right."

They let that sit there, the weight of the truths and untruths pressing on their legs so hard that they were unable to move. Ashley turned her face away from them, put her arm up and held her head in her hand, blocking Danny from seeing her clearly.

"I'm sorry," Danny said again, but it barely came out, stuck to their tongue like a cracker.

"It's fine," Ashley said, still looking off into the darkness beyond the stoop. "I'm fine." But her voice, they heard, was cracked.

SUNDAY

Rebecca snored in the passenger seat as Danny drove them back home. Ashley and Taylor had caught a ride with Rachel; Melissa and Lou decided to hit one more spring before heading home. It had been another late night, with an annoyingly early morning to avoid paying a late checkout fee. The friends had sleepily said their goodbyes, knowing good and well they'd all be reunited in a day or two, at the latest.

Finally, mostly alone, Danny thought about the night before, played it over and over again. It had been dark, but they could make out Ashley's shape; they felt her kiss their shoulder, they turned toward her. And then—they banged their head on the back of their seat. *What a fucking idiot.*

They had plenty of *good* excuses—they had been too drunk; Ashley had been too drunk; the cicadas had been too loud; they were turning into a lizard; their desire was too big, too monstrous, to hold, and just the idea of exposing it to Ashley felt too scary, too shameful. So they had rushed up to their room, pretended to be passed out when first Rebecca and then Ashley quietly lay down in their adjoining trundle beds—three sexless siblings clutching twin-sized sheets. Danny watched the light on the ceiling lighten as the sun rose.

The road blurred in front of them; their eyes stung. Their skin felt heavy, like they could feel it hanging off their skull, drooping. Rebecca's snores crescendoed, and they shook her shoulder quickly, a tiny earthquake to shock her body into quieting without waking her.

It was just about one hundred miles between them and home—their garage apartment that they had cleaned before leaving for the weekend. They let that draw them closer: their clean sheets, empty sink, laundry folded and put away. They imagined the relief of a shower, lying naked on their bed, letting their tired and hungover body sink and sleep deeply. Less than sixty minutes before they'd drop off Rebecca, turn off their phone, and be held by silence.

The relief lasted five hours, before the pangs of loneliness pricked at the softest parts of their feet. Danny wandered around their clean apartment with nothing to do, picked up books and then put them back down, turned the television on and then off. When it started to feel unbearable, they texted Taylor, *Want to meet in Five Points?*

Yes, when? Taylor responded within seconds.

Now?

On my way.

They sat outside in a narrow but long courtyard with multiple fires each surrounded by mixed and matched chairs. It was quiet, even for a Sunday. Taylor and Danny's fire was the only one lit, the rest of the bar's patrons choosing to sit inside instead. The movie theater next door had just finished its last showing, and a few more patrons walked over for a drink before heading home. One of the girls closing up, when she saw them, snuck Danny and Taylor a bag of popcorn through the fence that separated the back entrances to both businesses. While they snacked, they drank fruity and carbonated wine cocktails—lighter than the beer and whiskey they had consumed all weekend.

"Should I text everyone else?" Taylor asked.

"Sure," Danny said.

"Even Ashley?" they prodded.

Danny's stomach dropped. "Yes, of course Ashley."

"So, nothing happened between you two? I thought I saw y'all on the porch last night." Taylor held an expression of faux surprise, waited.

"Nothing happened." Danny's face was hot.

"But you wanted something to?" Taylor asked.

"I don't know," they said. And then, "I'm a fucking idiot."

"Don't say that about my friend," Taylor said.

Danny let out a sad, pitying laugh. "Invite her," Danny insisted. "We're fine."

They were all there in under thirty minutes—refreshed from showers and naps and a change of clothes that hadn't been shoved at the bottom of a backpack. Danny was, once again, awed by the beauty of their friends, by their ability to make the quiet and dark courtyard surrounded by parking lots feel loud and full and good.

They caught Ashley's eyes across from this different fire, and she offered them a smile that they returned. She didn't come around to them, stayed on the other side of the circle, turned to talk to Rebecca rather than hold Danny's gaze. She felt farther from them than ever before, and they wondered if they had missed her, like a comet, and if they'd still be there when she orbited back, or if it would even happen at all.

Danny's hands were clenched, as if they were trying to hold everyone in place. They already felt a wave of sadness, of anticipated nostalgia for this time. Even while surrounded by their friends, they already missed the unwieldiness and stickiness of their bodies coming together like an octopus, each person a tentacle grasping outward. How could they ever again feel this big and gorgeous in their collective love for each other and the impossibility of being young and queer in the wildness?

Hunted

When I tell Joe I want mirrors that extend from the floor to the ceiling on every wall, including inside the closets and behind the appliances, he asks a reasonable question: "Why?" I do not answer, "So I don't lose myself," because it is not a reasonable response.

After the installation is done and I've sent Joe a tip and a five-star review on the app I used to hire him, I walk through every room in the house like I'm giving myself a tour. I go outside, close the front door and then open it again. There is an infinite number of me in every direction; the reflections double and triple themselves until my body is moving into spaces that my house cannot hold. I do not touch the mirrors because smudged fingerprints would ruin the effect. Instead, I take off my shoes and drag my feet across the carpeted floor. You know, to really feel the ground.

Twenty-two, racially ambiguous, recently singled, bellied, landlocked, patterned socks, frequent masturbator, nut allergy, trying to pin down homesickness so I can hold it in my hands, put it under a microscope, understand why my heart hurts.

I write this list alongside other biographical details onto one of the mirrors in the back of my bedroom closet with black and purple dry-erase markers. The words imprint themselves onto my body if I stand in the right place.

It starts with Narcissus. One day, he spots his reflection in a pool of water and can't stop looking at it. He falls in love with his own image, stops eating and sleeping. He wastes away. My mom tells me the story when I am young and spending too much time staring at myself. It is meant to be a lecture on the dangers of vanity.

"It's not good for young girls to look at themselves in the mirror," she says. "You'll get lost in there." I am standing in front of the bathroom mirror. It is freckled with dust and water spots. Mom stands by my side, and I wonder if she is looking for herself in my features. Do all parents notice the stark halfness of their children, or is it more noticeable for my mother? Did her Chinese genes invade my father's white ones, or did his colonize hers? I decide then and there that it's the latter; I am learning that is how the world works. My mom points at our reflection. "There is nothing real in there," she says.

At school, I search for a bathroom, any bathroom. If someone else is using it, I sit in a stall, and wait for them to leave. I flush the empty toilet. There is one bathroom in particular that I like. This bathroom has a full-length mirror, and after I flush, I stand in front of it and do the thing my mother told me not to: I look. Looking is seeing and searching at the same time.

"What are you doing?" It's Eleanor. We have a Victorian literature class together. She sweeps her blond hair back with her fingers in a careless way that makes my stomach lurch. Eleanor wears fruity lip gloss, and her eyes are green. She lines their lids with a brown pencil, because black would be too dark. Her light freckles look as if they are hovering above her cheeks and the bridge of her nose; she doesn't wear foundation. She's sleeping with Mark Robertson.

"Looking," I tell her.

"Looking," she echoes. Her voice is quiet and soft. She smiles, nods her head. I think I'm holding my breath—looking at her feels like I'm on fire. *I'm on fire.* She walks toward me, and I think she's going to kiss me. *I think she's going to kiss me.* She puts our hands together, my palms on her palms. *My palms on her palms.* She leans in so our foreheads are touching.

Our foreheads are touching.

We meet between classes to hold hands. I trace her palms with my fingers. I rub my thumb against her skin. Later, when I clean out my car, I will find golden strands of her hair in the upholstery. They will be tangled with my dark hairs, and it will make me cry.

"What do you think about?" I ask her.

"What do I think about?" She kisses my eyelids and I can smell kiwi on her mouth. "You," she says. "What do you think about?"

I think about the first summer I spent away from my parents. It's humid and always pouring. The rain won't break the heat, so the two dance with one another until everything is hot and wet, until it and we have given in. I spend most of my time sitting naked on top of my sheets. It is in this room that I first surround myself with mirrors. I find them at thrift stores and on Craigslist. I drive to the suburbs for estate sales. I pick up shards of a broken sideview mirror from the sidewalk. The glass cuts my hands, but I keep walking until I reach the water. I walk over forty city blocks in unsensible shoes. Mosquitoes bite around my ankles, right where my socks end. The whole time, I keep the shards of glass clenched in my sweaty palms. I look at my reflection in the shards. I puzzle my reflection together in the broken pieces.

I bring home my new acquisitions when I know my room-mates are at work or asleep. They are white girls with white boyfriends. Like my mirrors, I find them on Craigslist. We meet at a coffee shop to make sure no one is an ax murderer. They look at me curiously, and after a few minutes, one of them asks if I am an international student. I don't remember which. They blur together. Their blond bangs are cut the same, and they each tap the tabletop as though communicating in Morse code. My head spins with double vision. I try to blink them away.

Eleanor takes me to visit her family. It's a three-hour drive north, and we hold hands through most of it. Not touching her is difficult. The town she grew up in is small, and when we stop at the gro-cery store, I can feel their eyes on our hands touching, our mouths touching. Touching. I can't stop touching—she pulls away from me. "I'm sorry," she says. "This is new for me." But I need her to hold me down to the ground; I need her to hold me still. We shop for the rest of the supplies without touching. Avocados, tomatoes, chips, seltzer—I like the carbonation. When we look through the pile of oranges, our fingers do not flirtatiously find each other. We do not grab a single orange between our hands. We do not look up and smile. We leave quickly, with unripe fruit, and when the automatic doors open to the California heat, the words "fucking chink" are thrown out of a passing car's window and push my body back into the cool, conditioned air of the store. "Chink?" Eleanor echoes. She looks at me, maybe for the first time, confused.

Eleanor's parents, Cathy and Bennett, are a sweet but stiff couple in their early sixties. It looks as if Cathy is going to reach out to hug me when she opens the door, but then something stops her. Eleanor's father takes my hand between his own. "It's very nice to meet you," he says. I am the first woman Eleanor has brought home, and I feel their unease when she walks me to the back of the house, where we'll be staying. She has a canopy bed, and her comforter looks like a cloud weighed down by mountains of pillows. She pushes me down onto it, and I look at my skin against the whiteness of the blankets and sheets. It's browner, uglier than I remember. Eleanor falls on top of me, a giggle escaping her lips. I kiss her before another pops out, and when my hand disappears in her hair I feel an unbearable desire to hide my whole body inside hers. I allow myself to dissolve into the sheets. We sink together until a knock at the door reminds us where we are, that it is time for dinner.

"What do your parents do?" Cathy asks me. She's prepared a pot roast and mashed potatoes. I'm not sure which ceramic cow holds the salt and which holds the pepper. The food is underseasoned; my tongue wants something with bite, something my tastebuds can feel. I miss the grit of salt.

"My dad runs his own company," I say. "My mom is a nurse." There is a silent chorus of nodding heads.

"So which—" She says and then pauses. She spears a single green pea with her fork. "Which of your parents is—" She waves her fork at me, the single pea still intact.

"I'm not quite sure what you're asking," I say.

"Never mind, never mind. I lost the thought." She pops the pea into her mouth. "Tell us more about school."

I do not touch Eleanor on the drive back the next morning. "They liked you," she says to me. Both of her hands are firmly on the steering wheel. "I can tell."

"I liked them too," I say. It isn't a lie. Eleanor's father reminded me of my uncles, the sweet way their eyes tear up when they laugh after too much wine. I could imagine spending holidays in her family's large living room, helping her mother in the kitchen.

I could blend in if I wanted to.

Eleanor makes us dinner in my small kitchen. She laughs at the chicken towel rack I bought at a vintage store before we met. She scolds me, lightly, for not knowing that flour can go stale. "Grab some ice cream while you're out, too," she instructs.

Outside, I lose myself. I walk through the grocery store in a panic. I catch the glances of strangers walking down the opposite end of the cereal aisle and I can't tell if they see me. I stand in front of the ice cream freezers and find myself reflected. I trace my features slowly with my eyes, and then my finger, until my hand grows cold and numb. When a woman reaches in front of me, toward the door, she says, "Excuse me," and grabs a pint of coffee ice cream. I smile and nod, happy she sees me, but I'm distressed when her body blocks my line of vision. I lose myself again and it feels like a sharp pain in my chest, at my temples. I am relieved when I come back to myself. I smile again. The woman looks at me strangely. I don't have a cart or a basket, not even a purse. "Are you okay?" she asks. I can't bear to look away from my reflection. I watch as I inhale through my nose and exhale through my mouth. I feel my feet in my shoes, on the dirty linoleum floor. I am there, in front of me.

When I finally reply, "I'm not sure," she is already gone, walking down the next aisle, grabbing canned green beans or peanut butter or soap.

It's not until I get back to the house that I realize I'm empty-handed.

Eleanor's hazard lights are on, the car still running, when we break up. When she asks me *why,* I tell her the truth. I say, *I can't taste anything.* I say, *Your blond hair makes me cry.* I say, *The worst parts of me ache when I'm with you.*

When I get to my bedroom, I lie on my bed. Before Joe left, I asked him to install a mirror on the ceiling. *It's not a freaky sex thing,* I almost said, but I wasn't sure of that myself. I see my legs and arms spread on an indigo comforter and they're beautiful. This time, there are only two of me: the me on the bed and the me in the mirror.

We dance in unison; our arms begin above our heads, swaying to an inaudible beat. Our fingers tap, tap, tap, tap, tap, tap. *One, two, three, one, two, three.* As our hands move down the sides of our body, our hips sway. Our toes point and flex. The entire time, we stare into each other's eyes, intentionally staying together. Then, I move my head to the left, and she also moves her head to the left—now, our bodies are no longer in sync but splitting apart. When I roll onto my side, she does too. We are a fractured kaleidoscope. We move in unison until we're sweating and our comforter has fallen to our floor. Neither of us reach down to pick it up. We are no longer looking at each other, but we know that the other is there. She is not going anywhere.

I walk to the bathroom under the pretense of taking a shower. I strip. I start with my socks—today's are maroon, with white rabbits. I take the left one off first, then the right. My hands unzip my skirt, push it down past my hips, my thighs, my calves. My feet kick it off. I pull my T-shirt over my head and throw it into the sink. It is a white T-shirt, and I almost lose it inside the ceramic bowl. My underwear does not match my bra. I take them off too. I'm naked—we're naked.

As our naked bodies extend into space, I do not inspect but allow them to grow and multiply. I fill up the room. The tile under my feet is cold; my nipples harden at the air's chill. Everything is quiet. I break my own rule and touch the mirror closest to me. I touch the curve of my waist, give it a squeeze. I hear a moan and am not sure if it is coming out of my own mouth or one of the infinite mouths—how would I tell the difference, anyway? The moan echoes. It bounces around our bodies.

I keep touching. I move closer to the mirror and put the tip of my tongue to the glass. It feels like bubblegum. Soft, pink, sweet. There is a squeal. A sigh. The moan continues to bounce, and as it moves around the room it gets deeper, more honest. A voice asks if this feels good and another replies, "Yes, yes, it does feel good." Says not to stop. But I don't think we ever plan on stopping because there's something about the softness of our tongue and the coldness of the glass and the way we feel inside our body, for maybe the first and only time.

Happiest

When her father won the weeklong vacation in the office Christmas raffle, Emily hadn't been sure if, at fifteen, she was still allowed to be excited at such a long time spent with her family in a swamp state. But she didn't have many friends to miss in her neighborhood, or at school—her friends lived in the phone she kept in the front pocket of the black backpack covered in doodles drawn with Wite-Out pens. So she offered her dad a genuine smile when he announced the news and didn't say much about the plan after that.

Weeks before the family's departure, her mother, preemptively reeking of sunscreen, looked over her shoulder at Emily and asked, without pausing for breath between thoughts, "Are you excited? What ride should we go on first? I was searching the internet for more information on FastPasses!" Mom was in a lot of Facebook groups and online forums. There were whole threads and blogs dedicated to Walt Disney World: key information on the best order to go on rides, where to find certain characters for autographs, the best snacks to pack to avoid paying for overpriced park food.

"I guess," Emily said, as she watched her mom look through Orlando Groupon deals and the resort's website again and again.

"You guess?"

This was Emily's cue to feel a shame so heavy it must have been collective. Her mother's life had been difficult. She had done things, lived through things that Emily could only imagine. No, that was wrong—she couldn't imagine them at all. And while her mother could plan a lot of things, she couldn't plan a better daughter. At a young age, instead of playing nice with the other children in her mommy-and-me group at the library, Emily found corners to read horror and science fiction books she'd pulled off the adult shelves. When she borrowed a copy of *Carrie* from a friend, her mother looked at her, aghast. "What is that?" she asked, just as the pig's blood hit Sissy Spacek's head. "Pig's blood," Emily replied, flatly.

Emily was thirteen when her mom had Joey. He felt like a second chance for both of them—a gift that would allow them to go their separate paths and feel less guilty about no longer being able to see the other in their rearview.

The day before they left for Florida, there was a ketchup stain already set on his Mickey Mouse shirt. Emily held on to his chubby little hand in their backyard as he gave her a tour of the grass, and the tree, and the pile of dirt he had recently assembled. Joey had a big head, too big for most hats made for kids his age, and wide brown eyes that made Emily nervous when he set them on her. When she looked at him close enough, their similarities startled her. He was the only person in her family who looked like her, the only other evidence of the joining of their parents' genes. They both had a light brown complexion, both had freckles that spilled onto their cheeks like potting soil on cement. Emily knew she was supposed to be annoyed with Joey, like when he would cry when she tried to focus on her homework, or because of the new responsibilities she now had after school, but Emily loved him. He smelled like milk after she gave him baths. They giggled at the same parts of the television shows they watched together. He always made it until the very last page when she read him books before his bedtime, even if he struggled to keep his eyes open.

Their parents were fighting in their room and most of the sound came from Mom. Emily couldn't make out the words, but she could hear her mother's anger. It moved out of her body like water pouring from a burst pipe. Even when it wasn't directed at Emily, it still made her shrink into herself. It stained the air, made everything feel heavy, moved through every room and haunted the insides of cabinets, closets, and bookcases. Her father was always gentle, as though his tall frame held space for his frustrations, while Mom's were compacted in her tiny one. Emily couldn't hear her father in the yard, but she imagined him absorbing each of her mother's blows. Her brother didn't seem to notice, was just excited to hold her hand and feel the changing Chicago air. He was a winter baby, but he was learning to enjoy the warmth.

Joey saw a spider crawl up his mountain of dirt, but he didn't scream. *Look*, he told her with sounds that barely resembled the word. He tugged on her hand. "That's a spider," Emily told him. He mimicked her. *Spider.* "Spider," she said again.

Emily picked Joey up and hugged him close. His big head fit just under her chin, and she rested her cheek among his thick baby hairs. They were starting to look like hers, and she knew that when he was her age, the individual strands would be as thick and strong as dental floss.

The Polynesian Village Resort was supposed to be like Hawaii, but Emily's mom told her that Polynesia is made up of over one thousand islands. When Emily closed her eyes, she imagined the sweaty heat of Florida as something different, exotic. Their hotel room was full of blues, greens, and oranges that made her think of deep sunsets and deeper waters full of colorful fish and sea turtles. The hotel's pool even had a waterfall, made to look like it was coming out of a volcano. Sailboats floated in the water that surrounded the resort. Emily had never been to a tropical island. She shrugged off any misgivings she had about the man-made beaches built for white people to luxuriate in a colonial fantasy in the morning and stuff themselves with sweets and turkey legs next to fairy-tale characters in the afternoon. She accepted it all at face value.

When Emily walked around by herself, white tourists from Kansas and North Dakota came up to her and asked if she was a native, sometimes stifling a laugh and sometimes with the utmost sincerity. A native to where, she wasn't sure—to the cabanas, near the overly chlorinated pool? To the Oasis Bar & Grill? On their third day, when she didn't answer quickly enough, the white woman looked at Emily impatiently. A small kid stood behind her, with sweet whipped pineapple dripping down its cheeks and onto the neckline of its oversized T-shirt. "Do you speak English?" the woman asked, slowly, as if every word was punctuated with a period.

Emily rolled her eyes at her and her dirty kid, shuffled away and looked for her family standing in line for Mickey-shaped waffles and banana-stuffed toast. Her mother held Joey in her arms while he squirmed. Her visor was already on her head, sunglasses hung from her neck. Dad put his arms around Emily's shoulder. "This is pretty great, isn't it?" he asked her. She shrugged, but his arm refused to budge.

"Aren't you hot?" her mother asked. She looked Emily up and down, her eyes pausing on her ripped jeans, then scanned the room. When Emily looked around, she saw the posters of faraway places looking down on park-goers filling cartoon jugs with sugary drinks and squirting ketchup on scrambled eggs. Sometimes they missed their mouths and food fell onto the ugly tropical rug. She didn't think her mother noticed this because she was only looking around the room to see if any of the other families had bad daughters who dressed in black on family vacations.

"I'm fine," Emily said, but her mom kept looking around the room, and Joey kept squirming in her mother's arms, and her dad kept one hand on Emily's shoulder while he read the paper with his other.

"What should we do today?" he asked. It was an unnecessary question, unnecessary because everyone knew, even baby Joey, that Mom had already planned everything out to the last minute, that she had printouts in her purse, extras of everything (individual bags of almonds, bug spray, a small misting fan a mommy blogger recommended and that she found on sale, Kleenex) weighing her down. She never asked for help and was always frustrated at the end of the day because nobody had given her any.

"Epcot," she said

Hours later, Mom balked outside of Good Fortune Gifts in the Chinese Pavilion. The song "Reflection," from *Mulan*, followed them wherever they went.

"What do they think China is?" Mom asked. "One big fortune cookie?" Dad laughed, but her face didn't crack.

"I don't know what she's talking about. I feel at home," he said when she was out of earshot. "I'm half Chinese too, you know. He was repeating one of his favorite jokes and Emily's least. She couldn't articulate why, but it pricked at her skin, felt like he was taking something that belonged to her and sticking it on himself.

Mom wouldn't let them take any pictures—"This isn't China," she said, as if they had already forgotten—until Joey almost wiggled out of his stroller when he saw Mushu, a large red dragon, surrounded by guests. "A dragon named after pork." Mom rolled her eyes again as she struggled with her phone. Emily forced a smile while Joey squealed with excitement. He grabbed Mushu's nose and laughed.

"What were you expecting?" Emily asked. "How is it different from the rest of the countries? The hotel?" She reminded her mother that the food store at their hotel was called "Samoa Snacks."

"It's different," she said.

"How?"

"It's China."

Mom started to cheer up as they walked through Italy. Charmed, she splurged on a papier-mâché Venetian mask while Dad found them gelato. When they finally made it to Canada, China was completely erased from her mother's mind. Emily noticed that she even let Emily's dad reach down and grab her hand, that she let him pull her hand up to his mouth to kiss. Emily was not embarrassed by the sweetness in the gesture, just surprised to see something she reserved for movies and television embodied in front of her by her own parents.

That night, Emily offered to watch Joey, without being asked, so her parents could go to one of the nicer restaurants at the resort. She wanted to see if their intimacy would continue if nurtured—if maybe when they got back to Chicago they would love each other enough again.

"I'll take Joey to Disney Springs," she said, remembering how much Joey had liked the boat ride from their resort to the outdoor mall, how he had jumped up on his seat and exclaimed when a real-life bobcat walked over a resort bridge above their heads; the wildness of Florida couldn't be contained, no matter how much Walt had tried.

"I have my phone, we have our bracelets," Emily said quickly, before her parents could find an excuse. She held up her arm, reminding them that she basically wore a tracking system around her wrist, though one that also allowed her to buy food for the twenty-five-thousand acres that Disney had spread itself across. "We'll be fine. And back before it gets dark."

Emily wondered how Floridians could measure time passing; the stickiness of February felt so similar to the mugginess of July. Her birthday was right before Christmas, so she became accustomed to marking change with frigid outdoor air and the subsequent feeling of melting when she went inside. She associated bundling—both off and on, a pinkness on her nose and cheeks, watching her breath stick in the air—with growing older and becoming some semblance of a woman.

Joey, so good-natured, smiled at the older women seated in front of them on the boat. Sisters, they told her, from St. Louis, on an annual family vacation with their respective husbands and now-teenage children. They cooed at Joey, told Emily that he was a handsome, sweet boy—*Such a good personality! A little ladies' man!* Emily looked over to her left, noticed one of the sisters' teenage daughters. She was also wearing black, and Emily almost wished that her mother was there to witness her, but was also happy to have the view to herself. The daughter's nails were chipped, painted a deep blue with silver sparkles layered on top, and her dark hair was straightened until it frizzed, long bangs almost covering eyes that were covered in chalky black eyeliner. Emily wasn't sure why she waited for her to look over, but the girl didn't lift her lined eyes from her cell phone. So Emily chatted with the sisters, told them about her school in Chicago—that no, she didn't do many extracurriculars or have a boyfriend, but that she liked to draw.

She held on to Joey, her arm around his little waist, as they docked. He put up a struggle as she started to move him toward the aisle, clutched onto the side railing.

"No," he said, staring instead at the water wistfully. "No."

"Come on, bud. Let's get dinner and then we can go swimming back at the hotel." Emily tried to reason with him.

"No," Joey said, his chest pressing harder into the side of the boat, his little arm reaching toward the waves created by the other boats' wakes.

"You're going to fall in, baby!" yelled one of the sisters, with a laugh. Emily scooped Joey into her arms, his baby body still soft enough to nearly fold. He let out another vocal protest but acquiesced to his sister while she soothed him with promises of a mouse-shaped ice cream sandwich.

Stomachs full of cartoon-inspired sweets and greasy slices of pizza, Joey and Emily spooned on their parents' hotel bed while the blue light of the TV washed over them. Emily's nose nestled into Joey's hair and she wondered if she would always love her little brother like this, if the tenderness she felt for him would remain or if pieces of it would harden as he grew bigger, his legs and arms becoming gangly, his hair sticking straight up out of his head. Her parents were still gone, embracing the time alone, and Emily let herself fall asleep and dream in cartoons.

After the gator drowned Emily's brother at Walt Disney World, her parents barricaded them in their suite in the Polynesian Village Resort.

Emily thought about all the deaths she'd seen in Disney movies. Bambi's mother, the brother in *Big Hero 6*, Ellie from *Up*, parents more generally. They flooded her brain—animated deaths, one after the other. Joey's fit right in. She imagined his dark brown hair with a dramatic swoop, his slightly slanted eyes exaggerated, his brown skin lightened. The music is worrisome, a cello playing as the alligator's yellow eyes light up the dark water. The tempo quickens and the alligator, colored a deep green so dark that it almost perfectly blends into the navy blue and black water, moves toward Joey, who is picking up rocks, the water only up to his small ankles. The moon hits the scene and Joey sees the alligator, but too late. His death is quick and off-screen; even the sound of splashing water is drowned by the quick fade to black. Dad running into the water, his failed attempt to save Joey, and Mom's screams are not recorded. The audience does not see Joey's body at the coroner's office, does not hear that he had in fact drowned first as the alligator pulled him under the water. There is nothing animated about Joey's bruised and broken body on the cold metal table. The audience is not there, like her parents had not wanted her to be there. But Emily, unlike the audience, insisted.

They started with the couch, lifting it across the room to the main entrance of the suite. They pushed the coffee table over too, the TV stand too bulky for just the three of them to move. Mom layered cushions, blankets, towels, even robes onto the mountain of furniture. Useless, she knew, but she grabbed anything that wasn't nailed down. "Leave us alone!" Mom yelled over and over, her face so saturated with tears that no more would come. No one responded from the other side of the door, if they were there at all.

The media arrived thirty minutes after Joey was pulled out of the water, flanked by the hundreds of guests who had their phones ready to record. Mom and Dad were ambushed on the way to their car, bulbs flashing loudly along with question after question. The media focused on Mom: pretty, tiny, and foreign. She was trending, though oblivious to it; invisible people on social media who made jokes about her inability to read the warning signs posted around the lagoon. The press stayed outside the resort, their bright lights never letting the sky go fully dark. Despite requests for the family's privacy, the handsome men and women stood in front of the hotel and updated the country. When they found out her parents were not leaving, even as their reservation ended and their plane left without them, the media too refused to budge.

Mom and Dad cried, holding each other, in their room. Neither showered, nor ate, for what felt like weeks. In the movie, it would have been a slow-but-steady time lapse, but in real life, the seconds wouldn't budge. The three days right after stretched themselves into the horizon. When Joey wandered into the water, Mom and Dad were holding hands. Something in the air had truly bonded them back to each other. Emily could see it in their faces, a Disney-only kind of magic. She was on her phone, looking at nothing. Even when your brother doesn't die, it all blends together. All Emily knew was that she wasn't looking at Joey, that she hadn't looked until she heard her dad call his name. Too late. Joey was splashing in the water, two smooth stones at his fingertips.

When they finally slept, Emily broke the barricade, stole her dad's wallet, and left their suite. The fresh air made her eyes water and her skin tingle. Nobody noticed her. While her parents were plastered everywhere—newspapers, resort TVs, guests' cell phones—she didn't even have a name: *Joey Anderson was staying at the resort with his parents, Tom and Rachel, and older sister.* Not a single reporter mentioned that she was the one who taught him to look for stones back home in Chicago, that earlier that day she had showed him, again, how she could skip them across the water. There wasn't a word about the way he screamed with delight as each rock kissed the water one, two, three times before sinking to the bottom. Emily filled her arms with sweet candy and salty chips from Samoa Snacks. She bought three bottles of Coke and a magazine that didn't mention Joey because it had been published the week before.

She sat by the pool, its waterfalls still running, lights illuminating the volcano and the cement beach. The pool was quiet, families shuffling their kids to dinner, couples waiting at the park for the nightly fireworks to start. Emily wrapped a forgotten beach towel around her shoulders, not caring who it'd once belonged to, just wanting to feel the roughness of its fibers on her skin. She waited for the sadness to wash over her, but it felt more like sitting in a lukewarm bath, her fingertips pruning and the bathwater draining slowly, taking parts of her down with it. Emily hadn't cried yet, but felt something burning in her chest, felt it rise into her throat and her cheeks every time she felt the starkness of others' family vacations and the new hole growing underneath her feet and her growing desire to jump in.

After the gator drowned Emily's brother at Walt Disney World, her parents barricaded themselves in their suite in the Polynesian Village Resort. Eventually, management burst into the room, but Mom and Dad held on to the bedposts. When a security guard tried to pry Mom off, Dad tackled him to the ground. Everyone was trying to be understanding, her parents were told, but the room was starting to smell like despair, and they had other guests to think about. They couldn't let their grief seep into the carpet. *Do you know how hard it is to get rid of sadness once it gets into the water?* Still, her parents refused to leave the room, too afraid to go outside and see what the world was like without Joey.

Or maybe they just packed their things up and went home to Chicago, joined a counseling group, and eventually divorced from the stress of losing a child. Maybe Dad would let Mom stay in the house while he found an apartment downtown, closer to work. Mom wouldn't touch Joey's room, his toys out on the floor and the Mickey Mouse shirt, still stained, in a hamper in the closet. Dad's new apartment would be clean and affectionless, some might say cold, but he would just say easier to keep up with.

Emily went back to the hotel room and stuffed the rest of her clothes into a backpack. Her parents were still huddled under their fort of misery and didn't notice as she took the rest of the vacation cash from her mother's purse and walked back out the door. She'd go southwest first, maybe to the Green Swamp Wilderness Preserve that she'd found on her phone or even farther, to the Gulf. She drew a crude map on a cocktail napkin and marked the springs where she'd be most likely to see manatees. In the winter, she had read, the giant sea cows come in from the ocean because the spring water is seventy degrees year-round. Emily would first learn to catch lizards and then to wrestle alligators in the Everglades, find enough smooth stones to fill Joey's old room in Chicago. She'd get boiled peanuts at every stand on the side of the road, avoiding the ones marked with Confederate memorabilia. She'd collect mosquito bites on her ankles at dusk and connect them into understandable constellations at dawn. She didn't know if the world would remind her of Disney World, or vice versa, but she'd eventually come back and find Joey's ghost. They'd talk about how sometimes you can't go home—not after the whole world breaks open, and you see that everything is haunted. Even your own goddamn body.

A Small Apocalypse

If she hadn't turned on the news, listened to the radio, or scrolled through her Facebook feed, she'd have no idea that a Category 5 hurricane named Percy was only a day away from the ticket booth of the small Florida movie theater where she worked. Melissa was selling tickets for the newest remake of a horror movie—first made in the 1980s, then the early 2000s, and, most recently, now. There was also a television version, but a customer told Melissa that it wasn't any good and she shouldn't bother seeing it. "I wouldn't dare," she assured him.

Melissa liked to tell her friends that if a zombie apocalypse ever happened she would just give up. "I'm not really interested in all that trauma," she told them matter-of-factly.

"But we'll need you," Rebecca had once told her, during that weekend trip they'd taken for Danny's birthday. They'd spent two days swimming and drinking and then drinking more, into the night, around a fire. "For the resistance!"

"I'll give the resistance a month," Melissa said. "If there's no sign of it ending after that, I'm done." And that was that. She could not and would not be moved from her opinion. She was like a big fat boulder with less than half of its mass aboveground; she was rooted into the earth. Melissa was not made for things like zombie apocalypses.

The theater was small, only two rooms that held one-hundred-and-fifty people, and fifty people, respectively. The new-old horror movie was playing in the larger theater. Melissa's manager told her to keep the main doors closed, to let the patrons form a line before letting them in the theater. There were many good reasons to do it this way, but patrons continued to come up to the ticket booth and roll their eyes at Melissa when she told them the doors wouldn't open until ten minutes before the movie started.

A line started to form, surprisingly headed up by a group of senior white couples who looked like they might be lost.

"Can I use your bathroom?" one of the women asked.

"I'm sorry, ma'am," Melissa said. "I can't let anyone in until the doors open. Both the coffee shop and the bar next door have restrooms you can use."

"Are you serious?" one of her friends asked behind her. "You can't be serious."

The line, already annoyed, was now irate. They joined forces against the injustice of the closed doors.

"I'm sorry. I really can't open the doors. Like I said, there are a few public restrooms available right next door."

The line was furious. The woman who needed to pee stomped her feet all the way to the closest bathroom, and Melissa swore she could hear her slam the stall door behind her once she found it.

"Absolutely ridiculous," the line said. "You have to be kidding."

As people joined the line, they were told the story of Melissa's tyranny. "She wouldn't even let a woman go to the bathroom," the line said.

Melissa found it difficult to count change with so many eyes on her, the line staring at her for another ten minutes. The line spoke about her loudly, knowing she could hear it. She gave one customer too many pennies and they kept them despite noticing the discrepancy.

"Would you ever get a tattoo?" the line asked. The line stared at Melissa's arms. "I don't think I'd ever get a tattoo." Heat rose up through Melissa's body; her arms and cheeks and ears felt pink and tender and visible. Like Asian glow without any alcohol, she would have joked with Rebecca, her only Asian friend in Florida. Melissa wanted to disperse her embarrassment, to share it with others so her body didn't have to hold on to so much of it.

"Hey!" a man of the line called out to her. He lifted his hand, *come here.* Melissa's face asked him *why;* she was not generally supposed to leave her booth and definitely wasn't keen to after her most recent interaction with the line, but the man smiled, waved his hand again jovially. Melissa conceded.

"How can I help you?" she asked. Now that she was facing him she could smell the beer on his breath.

"I just wanted to watch you walk out," he said. "Damn, you're sexy."

Melissa's smile fell from her face. She turned around and walked back to the booth without saying anything. A few minutes later, the man gestured to her again. Melissa shook her head no, aware that the line had now turned its attention to this new melodrama.

"Come see the movie with me!" he yelled out to her. His smile was big and goofy and he seemed to think it was very charming. She shook her head no again.

"I'm working," she said.

"But this is true love." His skin was blotchy and pink.

"I'm gay," she said.

"I'm into that," he responded. He winked at her, and Melissa threw up a little in her mouth. She almost opened up and let the mixture of bile and her turkey sandwich lunch fall onto her bottom lip and her chin and her floral tank top. Instead, she swallowed it, the doors opened, the line started moving, and she was alone again.

Melissa hadn't always worked in the small theater's ticket booth. She'd been working for the Center for Women only a few months before. She had liked her job and her clients liked her, were comforted by her, felt safe with her. It was her coworkers, first only one and then a few more, who had the problem.

"She said I discriminated against her because I said I didn't want to see a movie about a white man who saves China," Melissa told her friends, who had already heard the story. "If anything, I was discriminating against Matt Damon." There was a chorus of laughter, though her friends had heard this joke before too.

"You also said that all white straight men are rapists," Danny reminded her, though not in disagreement.

"Well maybe not all of them, but statistically—" she replied with a shrug. "Can you believe she had the gall to cry while she fired me? For discrimination? Like she gave a shit."

"They didn't deserve you, Melissa," Taylor cooed.

"Whatever, those nice white ladies can continue doing their nice white lady things at their nice white lady nonprofit," Melissa said with a huff. Her face was puffy. She had been crying. "If they wanted a fucking model minority they hired the wrong person."

"Clearly," Ashley said, leaning her head on Melissa's shoulder in solidarity.

"Antidiscrimination policy, my ass," she said.

"Want another drink?" Danny asked.

"Did you know one of my coworkers once described her eyes as chinky to me?" she asked them. Lou took that as a yes and ordered her another drink.

"Thank you," Melissa said. Tears were in her eyes, but she did not draw attention to them. "I'd also like a new job," she added.

"There's a sign outside the movie theater," Ashley told her. It was right next door.

Hurricane Percy was just starting to ravage Puerto Rico, and Melissa's Facebook friends were starting to pray, or at least say that they were praying, for the brown people they rarely thought about otherwise. A few posted donation links to the Red Cross, but most of them spent money on more bottled water than they would drink in months, let alone a few days or a week, plus bread, canned vegetables, and movie tickets. The water and the wind would hurt the people who were already hurting most, and it would keep coming into the month of October because who cares about the destruction of others once your phone screen goes black.

The sky was only just darkening, turning into a deeper, grayer, smokier blue that Melissa found beautiful. She would be able to see everything from her post in the theater. If the water from the river were to rise and come up Main Street, she would be one of the first people to know.

She had agreed to watch over the theater a few days before. The owners were evacuating to Atlanta, a seven-hour drive still in the path of the storm. Melissa's housemates were hosting a hurricane party. They bought a cake from Publix, a sheet cake decorated with shades of blue icing to look like a hurricane. A few bent plastic palm trees blew in the butter and sugar wind. *Take Me Away, Percy!* was spelled out in black. The housemates

had not custom-ordered the cake; Publix had been baking varia-
tions on the theme for days.

I'm working, Melissa texted her roommates.

But we're watching Showgirls, one of them responded in the
group chat.

And face masks, said another.

Sorry, Melissa said, and then she turned off her phone. To preserve the battery, she decided, even though the electricity was
still on and the theater had plenty of outlets.

Melissa loved to open the sliding glass doors of the candy display cases. The cloying combination of boxed chocolate and
bagged gummies and homemade brownies and Twinkies rushed
toward her face. She sat on the floor, rested her head against the
counter, and slowly opened and closed the cases' doors, letting
the smell flirt with her and then closing it back in. She loved
the movie theater now that it wasn't cluttered with customers:
babies reaching for popcorn with sticky hands and crying in the
middle of the horror movies, couples bickering about what kind
of soda they'd share in a single large cup instead of each order-
ing their own preferred soda in two smaller ones.

Despite the lack of customers, Melissa chose to screen movies
throughout the day, often with one in each theater. She stayed
on theme: *The Day after Tomorrow, Mad Max* (a double feature of
the 1979 and 2015 versions), *The Road, I Am Legend,* and *A Boy and
His Dog.* She wandered back and forth between the two rooms,
catching glimpses of the world ending, or people trying to survive after its ending, in each.

There was a lot of dirt in the apocalypse. There was some
crying, but not the kind of crying that Melissa enjoyed or found

cathartic. Melissa loved a healthy, long, and deep sob. She would sometimes hold in a good cry for weeks and then only let it go when her chest felt like it was breaking. She would contort her face into something so ugly and good and painful, let loud and bellowing and dramatic sounds fall out of her mouth. Her whole body would shake, and she would crouch and then curl into a ball so that her mouth would hit her knees and all the tears and sounds would bounce off her own body and hit her face again and again and again.

Melissa's kind of crying probably wouldn't be welcome in the apocalypse. Too much drama. Not enough dirt, not enough running, not enough logical planning. She was used to this—being too much and not enough all at once. It was a contradiction she sat well in.

She stuffed herself with popcorn slathered in nutritional yeast, garlic powder, and amino acids. Someone had hidden the bottle of truffle oil that she liked to spray on top in lieu of butter. Melissa was unsure if the bottle was hidden because it was expensive or because one of her coworkers thought it smelled like farts.

Popcorn fell on the floor. Kernels nestled themselves in the seats and got lost underneath counters, probably never to be found again. Melissa continued to refill her bowl; the never-ending snack coated her hands with grease and salt. Her bra would smell like popcorn and butter and smoke for days after. If there were any days after. Florida was not exactly her home state, but she had built a home among the heat, humidity, and swamp crotch.

Melissa had moved from Seattle, tired of the rain and North Face jackets and in search of something a little more, a little more—a little more *something*. There had also been a girl, a girl who Melissa felt strong love feelings for. Ashley had pulled Melissa toward Florida, toward this northeast city just south of the Georgia border. Ashley was lovely and tender, and she had sprouted from the Florida soil as if by magic—sundress and all. There had been about a year of domestic bliss, the promise of a one-day dog, and a yard that was always overgrown.

But Ashley had ruined things by breaking up with Melissa—not for any big reasons, just for lots of small ones—and then Melissa compounded the ruining by dating Lou so quickly afterward. It wasn't like she had invented the messiness of queerness, but there were moments when Melissa felt like she exemplified it. There were moments when the shame crept up from the ground and held her at the ankles, unable to move.

Still, Melissa remained dedicated to Florida despite its refusal of her.

"Move here," her best friend living in Philadelphia texted her almost every day. "I have an extra room and can help you get a job."

"I don't know," Melissa would text her back.

"What do you have keeping you there?"

Well, there's the theater, Melissa thought. *And manatees who swim in crystal blue water and alligators that hide in algae and sweet southern women who call me darlin' and sweetie when they hand me my change.*

"I'm just not ready to leave," Melissa said.

It was 2 A.M. when the power went out. Melissa woke up to the sound of wind pushing and pulling at the building, her body already missing the air conditioning. She found it hardest to sleep when her feet were too warm. She had fallen asleep in the balcony of the large theater on an old air mattress and the dirty pair of sheets she'd grabbed from her hamper on her way out the door. She fell twice, bumped her elbow and her toes three times on her way down to the lobby. *I didn't think this through,* she thought, stumbling through the dark without a flashlight.

Melissa looked out through the theater's glass doors. The street looked different without the light of the marquee. Clouds covered the moon, but small bits of light came through and she could see trees bending until they were horizontal and sheets of rain hitting the ground. There were no cars parked in front of the theater, no headlights illuminating the streets. For all intents and purposes, Melissa was completely alone.

It was in this almost darkness that Melissa asked her dead friend Rebecca questions: "Do you think I'm going to die in this theater?" she asked aloud. "Will the lights come on? When? Are there mice in places I can't see? Do you think I'm a bad person? Was what happened at the Center for Women my fault? What about with Ashley? Were you mad at me when you died? Did you think about me at all? Do you know how much we miss you? What's it like to die? How am I supposed to survive this apocalypse without you?"

After each question, she paused, but only for a second. The questions rushed out of her, so much easier to ask them as the pounding of the rain quickly hushed any other sound in its path. She could barely hear herself; instead, she let each word get swept away by the rushing water.

Melissa had hoped that talking to Rebecca in the haunted theater would make it easier for her friend to respond, that maybe in this spooky space there was some sort of portal to whatever dimension Rebecca was now in that would allow her to come back. Then again, maybe Rebecca hadn't considered Melissa that good of a friend—maybe she was only an acquaintance who'd dated and slept with two of her closest friends. Maybe Melissa's grief was overblown, outsized given the connection they'd actually shared when Rebecca had been alive. Why would a ghost haunt a friend of a friend?

When Melissa first started her job at the Center for Women she felt optimistic—bright and shiny, even. She worked directly under Greg, a gay man who wore a superhero ring on his right hand. He let the rest of Melissa's new coworkers introduce themselves to her during their weekly team meeting.

"Did anyone do anything fun this weekend?" Greg asked.

"I re-devoted my life to Jesus Christ," Vivian said. She had pearly white teeth and whiter shoes and was a recent graduate of the University of Florida. She was the kind of young woman who most everyone liked because she was thin, pretty, and nice in the blandest way possible. Melissa was already annoyed by her.

"Look," she said to Melissa as she passed her a tablet. "This is my lifestyle blog about being a newlywed, Christ, and party planning."

"Wow," Melissa said.

"I really love pink and gold," Vivian added.

"Yes, I can see that."

"Oh my gosh, your necklace is so cute," Vivian squealed. She grabbed the charm around Melissa's neck with her perfectly polished pink and gold fingers. "What do the scissors mean?"

Melissa's face felt hot—she was unsure of how to tell her new coworker for Christ about lesbian sex jokes and earnest lesbian sex and jokes about earnest lesbian sex. "I like to craft," she said instead.

Melissa, feeling some sort of kinship to Greg as a fellow queer person, felt comfortable enough during their supervisions to let some of her guard down. She told him about her life, her friends, even her family. When she made a joke about straight people, he laughed. When she found articles about the intersections of white supremacy and gender-based violence, he told her he'd read them eagerly. She built training curriculums about LGBTQ+ competency and antiracism; she brought up a need for nongendered bathrooms; at team meetings, she reminded her coworkers, endlessly, about pronouns. When they confused her, repeatedly, with another brown-skinned advocate, she let it wash over her. When the cranky receptionist told one of her clients that the "rape team" wasn't available, she tried to sit down with her and have a gentle heart-to-heart. The pay wasn't great, but it was the most she'd ever made in her life. The nonprofit swallowed her whole and spit her back out wearing an itchy turtleneck sweater and with just enough niceties to chat in the shared kitchen. She forgot and she forgave and she let herself get pulled under.

The water was starting to rise; the street outside looked more and more like a small river. Melissa wished she had looked up what to do in case of flooding. Her phone might still have some battery, but she had forgotten where she put it. She suspected it was under the five batches of popcorn she popped before the power went out. Why she popped five batches and why her phone was under them were unanswerable questions. She once heard to unplug all electronic devices and put things on counters or high stools. Common sense. Grabbing the keys attached to her waistband, Melissa unlocked the glass doors and made her way out to the ticket booth to save its computer. Wind hit her face before water did, but it didn't feel much different from the other storms she had walked into before.

Melissa wondered what Ashley was doing, where and with whom she was hunkered down. Ashley had kept the house, "kept" meaning she could still afford to pay its rent herself, while Melissa could not. Melissa had moved into a four-bedroom apartment only a few blocks away that was already inhabited by five other people. One of her roommates had chosen to move into a makeshift room in the house's foyer to save money and opened his room to her. It wasn't so bad, she told herself and her concerned parents over the phone, though he often had loud sex in the mornings, the thin bedsheet hanging in the doorway barely containing the low moans and groans of him and his various partners. Melissa missed her spacious house, almost too large for only two people. In her favorite room, the aptly named Florida room, she had put dozens of plants on tables and windowsills and floor. She had never been good at keeping plants alive before moving to Florida, but in this new room her plants flourished.

She was tired of the movie theater. Its expensive equipment, dark passageways, and ghosts closed in on her. The ghosts of the theater left no room for her own. One of the movie-theater doors suddenly swung open, and the wind claimed the poster of a small independent movie that nobody was seeing anyway. The floor of the ticket booth was wet, and Melissa grabbed the surge protector from the ground and unplugged each plug with quick precision. The booth smelled like a damp dog, but Melissa perched herself on a stool. There was a wide gap between the door and the floor, and a smaller opening in the glass window so Melissa could exchange money for tickets. The ticket booth would be a goner if the water continued to rise. The plugs would get wet even on higher ground.

She felt comforted by the marquee letters, neatly organized in alphabetical order. She thought about all the messages she could write, the way she could light them up once the power was on:

REVERSE RACISM ISN'T REAL

IN THE END, MOURNING IS COLLECTIVE

NOW HIRING: SOMEONE TO HOLD THIS REGRET WITH ME

I'M SORRY

NOW PLAYING: RAIN MAN

On her stool, Melissa watched the water rise around her. It couldn't touch her feet, but she thought about how babies can drown in only two inches of water.

They brought her in at 8:30 A.M. to fire her. Fresh off an overnight shift.

Why do I always feel like I'm in trouble? she texted a friend the night before.

Childhood trauma, Taylor responded.

"You have made some offensive and discriminatory comments to your coworkers," Stephanie, the codirector, told her.

"What exactly did I say?" Melissa asked. Stephanie and Greg looked at each other but didn't respond to Melissa's question.

"We're going to have to let you go," Stephanie said shortly.

"But what did I say?" Melissa asked again. She did not move from her chair. She wanted to laugh in their faces. She could feel a big, booming laugh rise up into her belly. She clenched in order to suppress it. She tried to make eye contact with Greg, her ally, but he refused to take his eyes off his stupid superhero ring. Melissa could see that there were tears in Stephanie's eyes, her whole face watery and red.

"I always cry when one of you cries," Stephanie said.

"I'm not crying," Melissa responded, though she could feel her own tears coming, as if to spite her.

Greg remained silent as he watched her pack up her things. Stephanie, unable to bear it, had stayed in her office. "Thanks for everything, Greg," Melissa said as she put a plastic mermaid she had gotten at Weeki Wachee Springs and a dim sum calendar her mom had sent her into the oversized purse she had bought just for the job. When she got in her car, she pulled off her sweater; she wore nothing but her bra on the drive home while angry tears blurred her vision.

If Melissa had learned anything from her movie marathon, it's that apocalypses come in all sizes and shapes—something for everyone. People would lose their homes, their businesses, everything they owned because of Hurricane Percy, and then there would be other hurricanes in the future just as there had been other hurricanes in the past.

She watched the water reach and then swallow her shoes. Her socks and leg hairs were soaked. The air around her was warm, but the water was cold. Her brain kept telling her to move, to go inside the theater, to find her phone underneath the popcorn—to do something. But Melissa did not budge. It was like those moments when she would get out of the shower and sit on her bed, naked, for over an hour, her comforter soaking up her damp body. She sat in the ticket booth and let the water rise, covering her shins and then knees and then waist.

Rebecca would have been indignant on her behalf, would have offered to pull up to the Center and throw toilet paper, or eggs, or paint, or years of bottled-up resentments. Maybe, selfishly, that's why Melissa missed her so much. She wanted someone to spit her rage with, to be consumed by fire alongside her. But, for now, there was only water.

Finally Melissa half-walked, half-swam back to the main doors and away from the ticket booth. The flooding hadn't yet climbed the sets of stairs, so the concession stand remained intact. Everything from Melissa's chest down was wet. She grabbed a Twinkie from the case, threw its saran wrapping into the water, and stuffed the whole treat into her mouth. The sweetness hurt her teeth, but she disrobed another, and then another.

She lay flat on the counter that on busy days was full with customer drinks and buckets of popcorn. On her back, she closed her eyes, opened her mouth, put her hand to her diaphragm, and screamed. It was a howl, it was a moan, it was a cry. It was loud enough to cut through the rushing sounds of water. Loud enough to wake a ghost.

Paper Wasps

Lily crushed the paper wasp's body with the sole of her pink tennis shoe, heard the crunch from the impact of the rubber on the glass window. It was the third wasp of the day, one of a dozen from that month alone. She always heard the wasps first, their buzzing louder than a fly, and their bodies bumping against the glass, trying to escape. Jenna tried opening the windows for them, opening the doors, but they never flew out. Lily reached for her shoes, from the rack near the front door, and swung.

Her dogs, one medium and one small, would sit still on the couch or the large cushion they shared on the floor. They would stare at her, wait for the swing to be over, for her voice to turn cheery and kind when she'd say, *It's okay*, and they would wag their tails and wiggle their bodies over to her.

"What does it feel like?" her therapist asked. "When you successfully kill a wasp?"

"Satisfying."

"How long does that feeling last?"

"Until the next wasp."

"And how does it feel then?"

Maddening.

When she knew Jenna wasn't around to hear, Lily would scream. She'd let out a primal yell so loud it echoed in their underfurnished living room. It wasn't just the wasps, either—it was the flies too, and the mutant spider crickets invading their basement. Her left eye twitched. She howled in the damp underbelly of their home.

"I just don't want them in my house," Lily said. "I can feel them—crawling on my skin." She demonstrated this to her therapist by walking her middle and pointer fingers up her arm like a pair of legs; the soft touch of her fingers on her skin made goosebumps rise to the surface, the thin hairs on her arm popping up.

Their house was almost too big for just the two of them, a two-story brick house in a neighborhood of old, big houses. Their next-door neighbors had four cars, each with a God-related vanity plate—two schoolteachers, who always remembered the names of Lily and Jenna's dogs. The house was warm in the summer, cold in the winter; vines grew through the glass windowpanes of the sunroom, spiders sewed their webs in almost every nook and cranny of the house. They had lived there for five years, had filled each room with throw blankets, heavy cedar trunks, candles, books, branches of driftwood—yet there was still an emptiness that followed Lily from room to room.

Every night before she went to sleep, Lily turned all three locks on the front door and then turned the front doorknob five times, each time pulling harder to make sure the door was really locked. Lily would then repeat this at the back door, and then the door leading down to the basement, and, finally, the glass door to the sunroom. She folded the blankets they kept downstairs on the couch, put two pillows on each end, then checked each door one more time, looping around the first floor like a ghost pulled on a string in a haunted house.

By the time Lily was done with her ritual, Jenna would be on the edge of sleep, the lamp by Lily's side of the bed still on, the dogs in their respective beds. It was then that Lily would draw, pulling her knees close to her chest and using them as if they were a table. She tucked markers and pens in the quilt, made sure that their caps were secure unless they were in her hand. She drew vines that grew from the sky, mountain ranges, ferns. She liked when the smallest part was the same shape as the biggest—fractals. She drew paper wasps as big as buildings, as big as people, standing on two legs and wearing open flannels over band T-shirts.

Lily would draw until Jenna, rolled tightly in the sheets, her eyes sleepy and barely open, said to her, "It's time to go to bed now, love." Jenna's arm would break through the sheets, touch Lily's still-scribbling hand. Lily would glance at Jenna, the paper in front of her covered in black marks.

"Okay." She'd put the paper and pens in the drawer of her nightstand, kiss her lover's cheek softly, and brush her dark hair from her forehead, hot and sticky. Jenna ran hot, like a little oven. She turned off the light, pulled the covers over her shoulders, turned her body toward Jenna.

"Do you still love me?" she would whisper.

"Yes, baby."

"Are you sure?"

"Yes. Why are we whispering?"

"It just fits," Lily said. Her voice would be low, her eyes open and drawing the shape of Jenna in her mind.

Sometimes, the wasps crawled. Lily would find her small dog in a play bow, her butt in the air and her nose to the ground. "Get," she'd say sharply, before grabbing the shoe or just lifting up her foot and stepping down until they were crumpled little paper balls.

It was October, just starting to get cold. Lily walked to work, the crunch of the brown leaves on the sidewalk reminding her of the crunch of the dead wasps under her foot, against the window. She paused the podcast playing in her ears, reveled in her own percussive music, walked in zigzags to stomp on as many leaves as possible.

When she got to her office, Lily powered up her computer. She clicked on the link to watch the confirmation hearing, a boy who was now a man trying to be an even more powerful judge and the girl now woman whom he had assaulted when they both lived in an affluent suburb. The woman, who had become a doctor, said she would never, could never, forget the way the man, then a boy, had laughed with another boy—what a good time they had with one another while she panicked, while she tried to fight them off.

Lily sat in her office, illuminated only by a small desk lamp in the shape of a pink flamingo, a reminder of the home and friends in Florida they had abandoned, the home they'd shared before the one infested with paper wasps. The morning was gray and dark; no sun shone through the office's window. Because her headphones were in and her eyes were glued to her computer screen, none of Lily's coworkers waved or stuck their head in her office as they walked past.

The question became whether a boy, now a man, should be held accountable for something he had done so many years ago.

"Yes," Lily whispered. "Yes, he should."

She drew pictures of the man, once a boy, colored his face with a red crayon, drew his mouth, big, and a paper wasp flying right into it. She drew pictures of the woman, her eyes closed and her right hand lifted, swearing. She was telling the truth, the whole truth. Lily thought about that—*whole truth*—thought of it like a stone fruit, a plum maybe, and so she drew that too, drew the men questioning the woman swallowing plums whole. Hard stone, soft flesh.

Paper wasps use their spit, and bark or parts of plants to make their nests—nests like paper bags. Unlike hornets, they are not outwardly aggressive, but they will sting you if they sense like their nest is threatened. They build their nests in trees, in the eaves of houses. Lily looked at photos of their nests online and thought about starting a papier-mâché project. She read that these wasps can be beneficial to gardeners, that they eat pests. She looked out through the glass sunroom door at the dead plants she had neglected, hanging from metal hooks. Jenna had said that they would try again with the plants, but Lily remembered they'd promised each other the same the year before—a perpetual New Year's resolution to better keep the things they wanted to love alive.

She dropped the glue traps down on the basement floor and then scurried up the stairs and out the door, out of breath from the seconds of exertion, exhilaration. She read, somewhere, that spider crickets jump directly at anything that startles them. Safe, back on high ground, she thought about the mess beneath her, thought about going back down to sweep up the dirt and dryer lint from the concrete floor. She thought about knocking the spiderwebs down from the ceiling. She thought about it, but kept the door closed behind her, already too tired, too overwhelmed by the mess. Wished she could simply will it, spider crickets and all, away.

Jenna was making a late breakfast—it was Sunday—in the kitchen. She looked up at Lily and smiled. "BLT?" she asked.

Lily smelled the bacon frying on the cast-iron pan. "Yes," she said. "Thank you."

"What do you want to do today?" Jenna asked. She was slicing tomatoes, cracking salt and pepper on each one. Lily loved this about Jenna—that she seasoned the individual tomato slices.

"I don't know," Lily said, before walking upstairs.

She tried to meditate, had downloaded an app on her phone, was using the free version. Lily sat on the bed she shared with Jenna, closed her eyes, crossed her legs. The medium dog scratched at the closed bedroom door, let out a medium-sized whine. Lily stayed put, kept her eyes closed, felt the softness of the blanket underneath her fingertips. She tried to deepen her breath, tried to not think about the dishes in the sink from lunch, the clean laundry that needed to be folded still wrinkled in the hamper, the recycling that needed to be taken out, the time she woke up to her once-boyfriend having sex with her, the prescriptions she needed refilled, the paper wasps bumping against the window.

"Baby?" Jenna knocked and turned the knob. The medium dog rushed in, wagging his tail and jumping off his back legs. "You okay?"

"Fine," Lily said. She opened her eyes, uncrossed her legs, welcomed the medium dog on the bed and wrapped her body around his.

"You want this?" There was a plate in Jenna's hand, the thick and salted sliced tomatoes on sourdough bread, layered with crisp bacon and arugula. She waved it in front of Lily, tempting her.

"Yes, thank you."

Lily's mouth was dry, but she chewed and swallowed bite after bite. She could feel Jenna's eyes on her while she perched at the foot of the bed.

"I'm fine, really," Lily assured her. "It's nothing that won't pass."

"Okay," Jenna said. She took the empty plate from Lily's hands and lifted up the gray blanket so that Lily could crawl underneath it. Lily grabbed the blanket in both her hands, crossed her arms to cocoon herself. She shut her eyes, though it wasn't even noon yet, and let herself fall asleep.

He was a nice man, nine years her senior. They had met when she was not quite twenty-one, when she was still uncertain of what it would mean to be fully herself, to let the messiness of herself roll over the containers she had built. When a man seemed good enough, even if not quite right. His big body barely fit in the extra-long twin mattress in her college dorm room on the nights when she didn't want to take the train to the apartment he lived in, with a regular-sized mattress and unwashed sheets. Years later, when she became his age, she tried to imagine lying with her twenty-one-year-old self.

They dated for one, almost two, years. Briefly they shared an apartment not far from a train stop and across the street from a bodega. He was a sculptor who teased her, gently, about her doodles. He would take her to art museums, going slowly from piece to piece while she rushed through, chasing her own momentum to the gift shop, where she would look at overpriced notebooks and expensive jewelry for someone else's eccentric aunt. He asked her not to draw in bed because the sound of her scribbling kept him awake and the ink stained his sheets. She let some of her softest parts absorb him.

One night, when she could not sleep because the buzzing in her mind was too loud, she watched a documentary about Sweetwater, Texas's annual Miss Snake Charmer pageant, a beauty pageant—no, scholarship pageant—in which the teenage winner reigns over the town's annual rattlesnake roundup. Lily played the movie on a low volume on her laptop so as not to disturb Jenna, sleeping a floor above her. The computer sat high on her chest while she lay almost flat on the couch, only her head elevated by the misshapen cushion. The pageant bored her—young, mostly white girls parading in formal wear—though she was glad when the only brown girl won. What really captured her attention was the end, when Miss Snake Charmer walked into a pit full of rattlesnakes, picked one up, and held it in her hands. In another scene, she chopped the heads off the snakes, and in another she gently, but forcibly, peeled their skin off.

When the snakes filled the pit they looked like a pile of earthworms, slithering over and around one another, all of their tails rattling, making music with their doomed comrades. Lily's skin tingled at the sight of them. Some of the snakes were irritated enough to strike, but their mouths met the hard material of bite-proof pants and boots instead of the tender, porous human flesh that would betray itself to soak up the rattlesnake's venom.

In the last scene, Miss Snake Charmer, after heroically beheading another snake, stamped her two perfect handprints onto a white poster board with the red of its blood. Around it, she wrote her new name in her rounded and neat hand: *Miss Snake Charmer 2017*. It was this scene that brought Lily to tears—they silently slithered down her face, the blue light of the screen illuminating their saline trails.

"What would happen if you didn't kill the wasps?" her therapist asked her.

"They wouldn't die."

"And?"

Lily held a yellow pillow on her lap, leaned against two more, as if her left side were being pulled down. The couch was full of pillows; there was almost no room for her to sit among them. Each had a different texture—velvet, embroidery, fringe. Lily touched them all during each session, but always held the yellow one on her lap.

"They would keep buzzing and bumping, they would take over, our house would fill up. They'd sting and none of us would be able to breathe—not the dogs, not Jenna, not me."

"Or," her therapist paused, "would they find a way out?"

Lily looked down at her shoes, hugged the pillow tighter to her chest.

"I don't know about that."

During the year she thought rock climbing would change her life, Lily told a coworker who also attended the gym about coming out: how it had felt like unloading a burden, how it felt nice to say, *I don't need to carry this anymore*. While they climbed closer to the ceiling, Lily told her about how some people would have described her as boy-crazy when she was younger. "It wasn't like desire, but something else, something desperate and sad," she admitted.

"Have you ever heard the phrase, you can't get enough of something you don't need?" her coworker asked.

Lily hadn't but had liked it. She put it in her pocket for later—a new thing she could tell people when they asked her if she'd ever dated men.

When it happened, officially, she remembered a friend of a friend drunkenly yelling at her, *Finally!* She was at a party with Jenna and this person started to chant *kiss, kiss, kiss!* She conceded, pressed her lips into Jenna's, and felt a pang of agony, of embarrassment, both for this friend of a friend who was being foolish, but for herself too, for not seeing something that other people so clearly saw in her. For taking so long to get there.

After the kiss, Jenna looked at her and asked if she was okay—did she need anything? Some fresh air? They went outside so the cool rush of nighttime air could rush through her head.

"Sorry about them," Lily said to Jenna.

"It's fine, babe." Jenna replied. "I like kissing you."

"You don't feel like you're on display?" Lily asked.

"They're happy for you," she said.

Lily was happy for herself too, but she held on to pieces of shame like broken glass in her hand. She remembered how, first in high school and then in college, she, filled with fear that nobody would ever find her desirable, or, worse, that her own desire would burn her from the inside out, flung herself at uninterested boys because that felt like the thing to do. And then, at this party, she felt herself flinging again, and that felt too familiar—like underneath the mask she had just taken off, there was yet another layer of papier-mâché.

Of course, he had not been the only one. It was not the only time. There was a small collection of boys and men who had come too close, who had crossed a line that sometimes Lily didn't even know she had drawn in the sand until it was trampled. These were not big events, not like they tell you on very serious episodes of after-school television. No, there was this time and then this one and that one—she could lazily count them on her hand. Moments that those boys and men probably never thought about again. Lily kept them, hoarded them—dozens of dead paper wasps, their bodies and guts smeared into a paper towel.

He was the nicest, though. He cooked her dinners vegetarian because he cared about animals. He picked her up after her last class got out so she wouldn't have to take the train home. When she woke up, him on top of and inside her, she didn't quite know what to think; his body was soft and warm—gentle with her, like always.

"Get off, get off, get off," she had said sharply. What had happened? He asked her if she was okay, reached around and held her. They fell back asleep.

In the morning, they tried to talk about it. "I'm sorry," he had said. "I thought . . . I didn't know—" He was having trouble putting together a full sentence.

"It's fine," Lily had said. "I don't want to talk about it."

So they didn't, though maybe she once in a while told close friends about how they had once started having sex in their sleep—that's how she had described it. They had both been asleep; they had both started.

He was a nice man, and Lily didn't bring it up again.

"Why is this coming up now?" she asked her therapist. "Years later?"

She was frustrated. Her therapist told her that her obsessive thoughts and compulsive behaviors were manifesting because she didn't feel safe. That she was checking the doors, the stove, the locks as a way to create physical safety when she felt emotionally unsafe.

"That doesn't make sense," Lily said. "It wasn't a stranger; it was my boyfriend, a person who I shared a bed with every night."

Her therapist nodded her head, leaned forward, parted her lips to start to speak—

Lily continued, "Besides, I stayed with him for a year after that. I didn't leave, wasn't upset with him. I slept next to him, slept with him. I laughed at his jokes, even the one about being Woody Allen and his Asian wife for Halloween. I cried when I eventually left him. I called him, months later, and asked for him to come back. So it's my fucking fault, my fucking problem, okay?"

"Do you really think that?"

No, but what if she had made it bigger than what it was? All of it. What if, even if she had been sleeping, her body had pulled him toward it—she would tangle herself up in the threads of not knowing and misremembering, and then she would be back there and it would be dark and she would be waking up.

When she got home she got a small can of black paint from the basement. She got the paint and a dried-up paintbrush, and she brought them up to her office, and she started to draw. To paint on the walls. She drew a wasps' nest, layers upon layers, lines upon line, some curved and some shaped like hexagons—space for the wasps themselves. And then, near the baseboard, she drew monstrous crickets, and even more monstrous spiders, some as small as her hand and one the size of a nightstand. She filled any empty space left with mouths, big mouths with lips and small ones painted black, like black holes with teeth, ready to suck and chew. She drew until the space was full and only she could tell where some things started and others ended.

By the end of November, the pests had retreated from the winter cold. Their large house slowly started to retain heat from the cast-iron radiators; their electric bill deflated for a moment. Lily had always preferred the cold, preferred to cover herself in sweats and blankets and let the small dog dig underneath the covers and warm her feet as it wrapped its body tight, like a cinnamon roll. She'd lean her head against Jenna's shoulder, will herself to not pick up her phone, to just focus on her girlfriend's shoulder and the episode of the television show in front of her.

She waited for a buzz, a bump, some critter or person to come barging through their door. When it didn't come—when the sky got dark and one episode and then another ended and it was still just her, Jenna, the small dog, and the medium dog—Lily's heartbeat slowed. She touched the soft fur on the small dog's belly, watched the medium dog sleep soundly at her feet. She listened to Jenna's breathing and matched her inhale, her exhale. And then again. And then again. And then again.

Beloved Flamingo Stoned to Death

When it was all said and done, the bird looked like a neatly folded tablecloth—his neck tucked along the length of his body, the black of his beak touching the base of his leg, a spot where his feathers bloomed from the palest of pinks to hotter and deeper tones. Lou was one of the keepers who had found him the morning before, crumpled and still. There had been blood, a pool of thick and deep red already staining the ground beneath him. The rest of the flock huddled away, restless and nervous energy surging through their own bodies.

It was only Lou's second full week at the Jacksonville Zoo when the three boys broke into the flamingo exhibit and stoned George, the zoo's oldest flamingo, to death. Lou had never seen a flamingo outside of captivity or their childhood lawn—their mom still stuck three plastic pink birds in the grass, only taking them in briefly to fashion small Santa hats on them before Christmas or for shelter when a large enough hurricane was coming their way. The flamingo exhibit was one of their first assignments for their internship, and Lou found themself feeling at home in the sea of pink necks and stilted legs.

George had fathered almost twenty children in captivity. One of his primary keepers, Jennifer, was a stout woman who'd worn a pink pompom in her hair every day since Lou first met her. "But George," she'd said, with a coo in her voice that was often reserved for babies or puppies, "was once a wild boy. Weren't you, baby?"

"Why didn't they fly away when the kids attacked them?" their girlfriend asked when Lou came home smelling like flamingo chow, which was normal, and with tears in their eyes, which was not.

"The zoo removes a joint in the birds' feathers so they can't fly," they told her. "It's called pinioning."

"That sounds horrible," she said.

"It's necessary to keep the birds safe," Lou responded with a shrug.

"Safe, like being stoned to death by deranged children?"

Lou slammed the bathroom door on their way to clean up. Even after a half hour in the shower, they still smelled like crustaceans, bird poop, and blood-covered feathers. When they slipped into bed later that night, their girlfriend turned her back on the specter of the stench and mumbled goodnight.

Their dreams were covered in flamingo feathers. They were in the pack of boys. The unruly group climbed the brick walls of the zoo, landed on their hands, cut up their still-growing palms. Lou thought that it smelled worse than the zoo animals, that stench of boyhood—tangy like vinegar, musty like sweat, saccharine like Mountain Dew. A thin, oily film on their skin as they sweat in the swampy, Floridian night. The goal hadn't initially been murderous; it was just to haunt the zoo at dark, to see what happened when night fell and families packed up their minivans and the moon came out.

They had all been told repeatedly, as children planted and watered in Florida, to avoid all lakes, ponds, swimming pools, large puddles—there was always the possibility of something sinister, like a gator, ready to drown your frail human body underneath the surface. But the black cement looked inky, and Lou worried that at any moment the ground would become liquid and they would be swallowed, first by the gentle wave of a lake and then by the jaws of a beast. They walked tentatively, on their tippy-toes, in zigs and zags.

They were surprised by the darkness; they could barely see. Then they spotted the bright pink of the flamingos, like glow sticks stuck into the mud. Their heads rested on their backs; Lou turned their own neck backward, mimicked the birds, and the other boys laughed. Lou didn't know any of their names but they all looked like the boys that Lou had grown up with in Tampa— still moon-faced, the tiny hairs on their cheeks looked like they'd be soft to the touch like peaches. One of them pulled on the pink feathers that started to sprout out of Lou's skin, stuck it behind his ear. Lou tried to laugh, but the plucking hurt them; their legs started to grow long and knobby, their nose and mouth hardened. First they had been a boy and then they had become a flamingo and then they were standing in the water next to George, stones whizzing by them.

There was a thump, and then a splash, and then uproarious laughter—and then Lou woke up.

Lou checked their phone; it was 2 A.M. Their girlfriend was asleep—her leg kicked out from under the covers, her arms clutching her pillow, her shoulders hunched. They closed their eyes again, tried to will their brain and body to fall back asleep, but their heart raced. They saw their own body, their half-human, half-flamingo body; it was bloodied and crumpled and pink and red like a valentine.

The autopsy was done in the morning, confirming what they already knew: George had bled to death. Jennifer petted the bird's head affectionately, told Lou about George's chicks and how they would sometimes nuzzle into her hair and pick at her pompom with their beaks when they were still young.

"What happens to him now?" Lou asked. It was far from their first death—a flash of Rebecca's open casket flashed in their head. That had seemed so barbaric to them. They'd felt too young to have a dead friend, to see her dead body on display.

"Stericycle will pick him up later today," Jennifer said. "They'll dispose of the body."

Lou's face was a question.

"A waste company," Jennifer responded. "It's protocol."

Lou tentatively touched the tip of George's beak, still afraid that he might wake up. He could bite them, he could be frightened, he could remember what had happened to him.

"I'm sorry, buddy," they whispered to him. They petted the top of George's tiny head, moved their hands underneath his body and lifted. George was even lighter than they thought.

It wasn't until they were halfway to Tampa with a dead flamingo in the backseat of their car that they started to doubt their plan. George was wrapped in a borrowed Jacksonville Zoo blanket from the gift shop, the price tag dangling off the edge of the seat. All four windows were rolled down, the wind blowing through the car and whipping at Lou's face. They put on a burned CD they'd made in high school and let it play in a loop for the three-hour drive—Rilo Kiley, Bright Eyes, and Death Cab for Cutie. It was comforting, knowing all the words.

Rebecca would have been the first person they'd have called, driving with a dead flamingo in their back seat. She would have met them outside her house, would have worn all black to embrace both the gravity and drama of the situation. Rebecca was the friend you could call to get rid of a dead flamingo body.

Lou's girlfriend hadn't known Rebecca, hadn't been a part of that constellation of friends and exes and other things in between. At first, that had been a part of her appeal. Their group was weighed down by grief, by breakups, by disappointments, by broken promises and trampled-on boundaries. It was nice to meet someone like her, someone with her own group of friends with their own bars and backyards and traditions. But there were also times that Lou missed the easy understanding of their friends. Rebecca had been their most annoying beloved: the first person to call them out when they were being a dick, the loudest objector to the three-month hookup with Melissa after she and Ashley had just broken up, the most controlling when it came to group gatherings or nights out. But Lou still, at times, couldn't reconcile being with a person who hadn't known her, hadn't loved her, hadn't felt her absence like a hole in the chest.

They thought about the summer after their second year of college when Rebecca came to stay with Lou and their parents on her tour of the state, a successful attempt at avoiding spending time with her own family. Lou set up their childhood bedroom for a weeks-long sleepover, pulled out the squeaking twin-sized trundle and emptied a drawerful of clothes they hadn't worn since high school. Rebecca put all her weight on her horn when she pulled into the driveway and Lou caught their mom tense when Rebecca ran up and hugged her instead of taking her hand to shake.

They spent most of their days in the lanai, a glass-enclosed patio with a small pool they could dip into when they overheated. Lou remembered Rebecca surrounded by diet soda cans and magazines, sunglasses perched on top of her head and stamps of her red lipstick on the plastic bendy straws she found in the kitchen and insisted on using. She weaseled her way into Lou's mom's heart by jumping up to do the dishes after dinners, neatly folding her clothes in the borrowed drawers and the sheets on the borrowed trundle every morning, and making her laugh. Lou took her to Raccoon's, the dive bar just outside their subdivision, and they ordered whiskey; they went to gay bars in Tampa to dance and they ordered Red Bull and vodka.

It was the first time Lou had ever spent with Rebecca alone. She was quieter, more apt to listen, when she wasn't fighting for attention in their larger group of friends. Lou had expected to be exhausted by her by the time she left, but instead they asked her if she wanted to stay another week, and then one more. Days after she finally moved on to visit another friend in Tallahassee, both Lou and their mom kept her bed made up, just in case.

Lou pulled into the driveway of their mom's house, everything already blanketed in darkness. Their headlights lit up the three plastic flamingos, one off-kilter, as if it'd been caught doing something illegal. Like deer caught in the headlights, the flamingos' painted eyes looked both surprised and frightened.

Their mom kept a shovel in the garage at the edge of their property. Mosquitoes bit at their elbows, the soft spot behind their knees. They buzzed in their ears. There had never been a lock on the door, or they had one once but had lost the key and had to use bolt cutters to get to the lawn mower. The family agreed not to buy another lock, not to risk the chance of losing another key; they didn't keep anything worth stealing in there, anyway.

The handle was rusted, the whole thing heavier than they'd expected. They couldn't remember if they had ever dug a hole before. Lou couldn't remember why their family had bought the shovel in the first place. Luckily, the ground was soft, and it gave way to the metal and the adrenaline that had been pumping through their body since they got in the car with the dead flamingo.

"Who the hell is that?" Their mom slammed the front door open, the wooden bat she kept underneath her bed in her hands.

"It's me, Mom." Lou said.

"Lou? What are you doing here?" She didn't loosen the grip on the bat, afraid someone was trying to trick her.

"I don't know, Mom," Lou answered truthfully. "Will you help me?"

"Help you do what? It's almost midnight."

"Bury this flamingo. From the zoo."

"Jesus Christ." She let out a huge sigh. She was leaning on the bat now, using it like a cane.

"His body is in the backseat." And they started to cry again. "I just couldn't—"

"Your dad bought a new shovel last month," their mom interrupted them. "I'll go get it."

Mother and child dug a hole, as deep as they could, measuring the depth with the length of the handles of their shovels. When it was deep enough, Lou's mom went into the house and came out with a clean sheet, wrapped it around the dead bird and the Jacksonville Zoo blanket that would not be returned to the souvenir store. They gently threw dirt over him, and then patted the dirt down, packed it tight before throwing more dirt over that dirt and then patting it down again. Lou hugged their mom goodbye, both of them sweaty and disgusting, promised to bring *that girlfriend of theirs* home over Christmas. Their next shift started in four hours and they had to shower, had to get back.

On their way home, Lou thought about Rebecca's funeral again. They thought about how they hadn't actually seen her body, how they'd only been able to catch a glimpse of the casket from the back of the church before they had to go outside to smoke a cigarette. When it was all said and done, their friends had spilled out of the church tear-stained. And Lou remembered feeling a sense of relief at the impossibility of ever feeling as useless as they did in that moment again.

Upstairs

She woke up to a shriek, to footsteps vibrating through the floor-boards above her and then stomping down the stairs that touched the outside wall of her bedroom. Streetlights shone through the spaces between the blinds, making the dark sky look bright—she still needed to sew a set of curtains, the fabric she bought six months before collecting dust in a closet. She looked at her phone: 3:47 A.M. A familiar rattling noise, like a dog pacing in its crate, started soft, but built steadily; she reached blindly to her right and found a shoe and threw it up at the ceiling. Her own dog cried in its bed before trotting to her outstretched hand and placing its head gently into hers. *It's okay*, she told it, feeling its soft fur and wet nose with her fingertips.

There were two distinct sets of footsteps, two tones and timbres of voices. The first was lighter—both the step and the voice—and harder to pinpoint. Maybe timid. The second picked up its whole foot before slamming it down into the naked hard-wood floor, its deep voice barreling into her apartment with clarity—*Fuck!* was a frequent exclamation. Both sounded like they enjoyed moving their furniture throughout the day and night—she imagined them dragging armchairs, armoires, chests full of gold bars across the floor. It was only in her small kitchen that she couldn't hear them; she resorted to putting a small chair in the middle of the room and curling into it when her left eye started to twitch from the constant noise. The buildup of the dishwasher became a white noise machine and she'd run it empty, or with clean dishes still inside, when she had difficulty falling back asleep.

He had moved out of what had once been their apartment before the new upstairs neighbors moved in. This, she was grateful for, because she could only imagine his rage, the looks he would have given the ceiling, his own stomping feet as he marched up the shared staircase to their apartment and knocked on their door. He would have complained loudly, acting out his annoyance at the apartment she'd picked out, conveniently forgetting that he'd been the one to suggest it. *Are you kidding me?* he would've yelled in the middle of the night. She was glad he was gone, glad he had left, though she wondered if these new neighbors were her punishment for her gladness, something he could inflict upon her even now that the locks had been changed.

Dear neighbors—I live just beneath you, in Apartment A. Could you please put down a few rugs? I can hear quite a bit through the floor-boards, and it would help me greatly if you could put something down to help muffle the sound. Thank you.

She left the note taped to their door, quietly running up and down the stairs so they wouldn't hear her coming or going. After three nights of no sleep, her skin felt like clay, thick and stuck to her bones. She could feel her eyes in her skull, straining to see clearly. Waxed paper cups and fast food restaurant bags littered the dining room table. Menstrual blood stained the white toilet seat. More clothes were on the floor and tucked into the folds of the couch than were in her drawers. Fruit flies convened on rotting bananas sitting on the kitchen counter, their sweet insides bursting out from their skins. The noise was constant: footsteps, alternately tense and boisterous conversations, a dog barking, glass crashing. *Please be quiet*, she whispered to herself like a prayer. It was 7 A.M. and it sounded like there was a small party above her; it sounded like the laughter was coming from inside her own head. Every time her eyes felt too heavy to keep open, a sharp and loud knocking against the floor startled her awake again.

Her note went unanswered.

His favorite thing to do during a fight was to grab her phone and throw it across the room. She'd watch it skip on the hardwood like a pebble on a pond. *Why the fuck is she texting you again?* he'd yell, a redness creeping into his cheeks. *Are you okay?* The message he'd seen was now barely legible through the cracks in the screen, lightning bolts in glass. The dog would pace in its crate, gently whining and making small circles on a blanket. *Do you think I'm a fucking idiot? That I don't know what's going on?*

The property management company responded to her email with a curt, *There is currently no tenant living in Apartment C.*

As she read the note, what sounded like a bowling ball rolled across her ceiling. She looked up and heard a laugh, this one sounding cruel. Someone walked down the stairs and she rushed to deadbolt the front door to her own apartment. There had once been a door chain, but he'd ripped it off the first time she tried to lock him out. There was a knock on the door, but she was too short to see through the peephole. Another knock, but whoever was on the other side didn't say a word when she asked who was there. The pounding felt like it was coming from inside her chest, like she had swallowed its vibrations and they'd taken over her heartbeat. She pushed a bookcase in front of the door and ran to her chair in the kitchen.

By the time she watched the sun rise, the dishwasher had completed five heavy cycles. Steam filled up the small space, but a pink and orange sky broke through the fogged kitchen window nonetheless. And everyone knows that the horror movie is supposed to end at daybreak—but the noise continued.

She held the dog's leash and a hammer in one hand and reached for the doorknob with the other. It turned with no resistance. The door whined as it opened. The dog rushed in, tail wagging in the air and leash dragging on the floor behind it.

Hello? Her voice echoed in the empty apartment, seemingly identical to her own, though with more natural light. No one responded. She opened each closet, looked in the pantry twice and then once more. It was just her, the dog, and the hammer in her hand. And then she heard it—the voices, the steps, a scream. She lay down on her side; she put her ear to the hardwood. The dog put its head on her hand, whined softly. *Shhh*, she told it. There was a muffled yell, a slammed door.

They were downstairs. They were inside. She could hear them.

Three-Card Spread

PAST: EIGHT OF CUPS

Walk away, leave, move on.

He knew even before he heard his uncle's drunken jokes, could feel it in each layer of his skin, in the weave of his muscles, in his bones. He knew he was some kind of freak. When he inspected his naked body in the mirror, he couldn't see much that was physically different from the other boys at school. He counted his toes (ten), his fingers (ten), his balls (two), his belly button (one, an innie). He had dark hair and his eyes were slanted, and his nose was on the wider side, but his dad had those things too. And Arthur had seen photos of dozens—no, thousands, or even more—of people who looked more like him than like Danny or Chad or Rhett.

What was wrong wasn't something just anyone could see, but it was something most people could feel, if they paid enough attention. Luckily for Arthur, most people didn't pay him any;

they were too absorbed in themselves. But, even so, people tended to stay away from Arthur Zhao. It wasn't because he was the only Chinese boy in his grade or because his family was one of what seemed like only a handful of Asian families in town. This didn't help, but Curtis Tokushige was popular enough, especially now that he played shortstop for the JV baseball team. Everyone—not just Arthur's classmates, but his teachers too—stayed what felt like six feet away from Arthur. If you were to ask anyone why, no one could explain it. A quick look into his dark eyes seemed to make people nervous and skittish, so Arthur started to keep his eyes downcast, to follow his shoes while he walked. He didn't blame them; if it were at all humanly possible, he'd have jumped out of his own skin and run away from himself too.

It wasn't until he heard his Uncle Tai, drunk off the cheapest wine Arthur's mother could find, laughing so hard at his expense that all the pieces fell onto the soiled carpet and into place.

"We should get one of those documentary crews to come here," Arthur heard his uncle's loud voice filling the living room, making its way through the kitchen and down the hall into Arthur's darkened bedroom. "White people love murders. Arthur Zhao could be the most famous of all! Killed his brother in his mother's womb. A killer before even receiving the gift of life."

Arthur's mother tried to hush her brother-in-law, but Arthur could hear his own father chuckling quietly. "Now, Tai, you know my wife is superstitious. Don't upset her."

"I'd be superstitious if I were her, too," Tai wailed theatrically. "Twins? Good luck. A blessing on the whole family. But whatever Arthur is—" Arthur imagined his uncle waving his hand, miming the act of throwing something away. In his imagination, his uncle's face was distorted into a clown-like frown.

Arthur's heart, which had sped up as he secretly listened in on his uncle and parents, suddenly skipped a beat. *Bu-bump-bu-bump-bu—*. He held his pointer and middle fingers to the nape of his neck and felt it. *Bu-bump-bu-bump—bu—bu—bu.* And then, he wondered, could he feel, no, but maybe? Two heartbeats? *Bu-bump-bu-bump-bu-bump-bu-bump.* No, it was just a trick of his own cruel imagination.

A few nights later, when Arthur's mother was putting him to bed, he got up the nerve to ask her, "Ma, is there something wrong with me?"

Dread flashed across her face, but he saw her wrestle it down with a quickness that comforted him. "No," she said sternly. "Why would you ask that? Do you not feel well?"

She went to touch his forehead, an empty gesture. He knew that she knew that's not what he'd meant.

"I'm not sick," he said, though he did not say that he was well, or fine. When she withdrew her hand, it pained him. Even then, he knew that touch was scarce.

"What did you and Uncle Tai talk about? With Ba?" he asked more clearly.

"Your uncle in an idiot," she said. "You know that."

"But is it true?"

He hoped she wouldn't make him say it out loud, that she would stop her side of the game.

"It's true," she said. She sat on the edge of his bed, perched. She looked like a crane, her neck long, her eyes dark and sharp. "When I found out I was pregnant, there were two heartbeats, but a few months later, there was only one." She paused, held

Arthur's eyes with hers. "But that has nothing to do with you. You are a good boy. A good son."

Arthur met Zoe when he was twenty-six. They were both graduate students at Berkeley—he in comparative literature and she in ethnic studies. It was his second year in the program, and all he wanted to talk about were ghosts and Derrida; Zoe found herself to be both enraptured and frustrated by the shy, wispish man who asked her deep questions about her research while not at all understanding the collages that she made on her computer with layered videos, sound, and photos, often of his face, his hands, his voice. "It's about racial melancholia and preemptive homesickness. It's about US imperialism, about the impacts of technology on our bodies," she told him.

Arthur intrigued Zoe, and she was the first person since his mother to sit so close to him, to push his hair out of his eyes and see something other than darkness. She was short, but he would not describe her as tiny. Her wide shoulders were built for something like gymnastics, and her thick long hair would take up almost half the small bed that they shared if she didn't keep it pinned up in a dutiful twisted knot. Zoe took up space in a way that brought you closer to her. After he first met her, he waited for her to get the chill, for her anxiousness to grow between them. Then, they slept together once, and then another time, and then often. He waited again for her to leave, to hear stories from friends of friends about how he was a creep.

Instead, they found an apartment to share. Zoe commenced what she called nesting, dragging Arthur to flea markets and thrift stores to buy mismatched plates, bright ceramic lamps, tapestries, and cloth placemats she promised to turn into throw pillows for their couch. And as their shared space filled with things, Arthur felt a type of wholeness, a groundedness. In their bed—a second-hand futon that they never folded into a couch—they spent mornings drinking tea and reading novels; Zoe made it a rule that they could read only novels in bed. Journal articles and academic papers were exiled from the bedroom. It was on one such morning that he told her.

"What's the weirdest thing about you, do you think?" Arthur asked.

"Weird? I'm sure there are lots of things about me that other people think are weird," she said. "I don't know if I give it much thought."

"Okay, not weird, then. Beyond weird. What is a word for something beyond weird?"

"It depends. Grotesque? Horrifying? Bizarre?"

Arthur nodded, his brow furrowed.

"Okay, why so serious, honey?" Zoe said with a performative lightness. She nudged his arm with her big toe.

"Don't you ever wonder why your friends haven't warmed up to me? Why I don't have my own friends? Why people cross the street when they see me?"

"Arthur," Zoe said. Her voice was gentle. "That's not true. My friends like you just fine; it's not that you don't have friends. You're just shy—introverted."

"I am grotesque," Arthur said, his voice taking on an echoed quality. Like two voices speaking in perfect, subtle harmony.

"Baby—"

Arthur kept his eyes downcast on the sheets, his legs folded beneath him.

"I am half ghost," he told her. "I am death, I am the reaper and the reaped."

He could feel Zoe's heartbeat quicken, watched her tense, saw her instinct to leave their bed flash in her eyes and across the surface of her muscles. She twitched.

"I am half ghost," he repeated. "I am the murdered and the murderer."

"Arthur," she said slowly.

"I'm not just Arthur," he said. He covered his face with the flat sheet. His cries were muffled, his tears starting to poke through the fabric.

"That's okay," Zoe cooed. "You don't have to be just Arthur. Who else are you?"

"They didn't name me."

Zoe folded him into her arms like a blanket.

"Do you think my mother grieved him?" he asked, his voice muffled by the softness of her skin.

And even though she didn't know exactly who he meant, she said yes.

The first few months of Wanda's life, Arthur barely put her down. She ate, slept, and shit in his arms, and he lapped it all up, like it was honey. He read about skin-to-skin contact and unbuttoned his shirt so the soft, plump skin of his daughter could touch his; he let Zoe sleep and eat and take baths; he kissed Wanda's forehead and then Zoe's and called them "his girls." Arthur was a beam of light.

And in those months, people talked to him—came up to baby Wanda and cooed at her, asked him how things were going and seemed interested in his answers. Wanda filled all the empty holes that were inside of him and he was at once a good man, a good father. If his Uncle Tai were still alive, if he hadn't drunk so much his liver was practically pickled, Arthur would have taken

Wanda to him. He would have presented her on a silk pillow and said, "See, look at the beauty I can make."

Still, sometimes it would sneak up on him—the doubt, the grief, the emptiness. He'd look at Wanda's face and wonder who she looked like. He'd ask, "Whose nose do you think that is?"

And Zoe would say, "It's your nose, of course." She'd lift Wanda up in the air and kiss her button nose that at first looked like Arthur's, but then didn't, not at all.

"And what about her ears?"

"Mine," Zoe would say, her voice light and sweet and crisp.

"Her eyes," Arthur asked then, only a hint of desperation on his tongue. "Whose eyes?"

"Those big, beautiful, dark-brown eyes?" Zoe sang. "Those couldn't be anyone's eyes but yours, my love."

Wanda was eight when Arthur left. Old enough to remember him, he thought, and young enough to maybe not resent him for making her. Most people wouldn't understand, would see him as cruel and selfish, but he was worthless to her, barely a father. Zoe would be fine without him. She had just received tenure in the English department at the University of Florida, an attempt to inject color into their mostly old and white department. She could afford their modest home on her own salary. She had told him about her new friends at work, how she liked the woman who lived next door. He reasoned with himself that she would have the support she needed.

He heard there might be others like him, maybe in Texas or upstate New York, somewhere near a border, where people were familiar with an unnatural force imposing itself on their bodies and minds. In California, and then again in Florida, he had gone to doctors who told him that, while rare, the events preceding his birth could not have physical effects. A psychiatrist medicated him. A therapist told him to meditate, to quiet his mind. Nobody would listen when he told them he could feel the presence of his dead twin inside of him, that his daughter did not feel like his child, that there was something off, about both of them, no, all three of them. He tried to tell Zoe, but she told him, "You're scaring me." She said it over and over like a prayer. She blocked him with her body so he could not get to Wanda's room, but he did not want to go in there; he wanted to get as far away from her, from them, as he could.

He bought a used car from a lot for $1,000 in cash. He packed a small bag of his things and left everything else for Zoe, for Wanda. He drove southwest first, just on a hunch, to Ponce de Leon Springs. What could it hurt, to try the healing spring waters that were said to provide eternal youth? That, of course, was not what he was after, but if there was some sort of magic in those waters he wanted to swim, to soak, to drink every last drop up.

PRESENT: TEN OF WANDS

Carry, burden, break.

Wanda Zhao logs into her Zoom account, clicks the link in her calendar that takes her to a virtual waiting room. It is only her second support group meeting. She is almost thirty, a few months shy of her birthday. She wasn't sure if she would like processing in a group, but her therapist and Grace had encouraged her to try, and her mother had shrugged and said, "What could it hurt?" without ever turning to face her. The first meeting had been fine; Wanda had mostly listened, had only introduced herself once. There were people like her all over the country, she had learned, and that felt good enough.

She likes looking at the other disembodied faces on the screen, but hates seeing her own face reflected back at her. Her camera is turned off so she can avoid fidgeting with her hair or looking into her own eyes. She puts the speaker in the main view, focuses on their face and wonders how much they ruminate about their own. Phillip, a white man, probably only twenty-four, seems the most confident. His camera stays on, a ring light illuminating his beautiful features; he doesn't blur his background, nothing to hide. Wanda thinks about him between sessions, even says his name out loud to herself while she washes the day off her face before bed. She wonders what it would be like to be Phillip, to keep your camera on, to feel so compelled to talk about your experiences. Wanda is almost glad for Phillip; if he wasn't an adult child of a disappeared twin there would be nothing interesting about him. And then Wanda wonders if the same could be said about her.

Her mother never talks about her father, not even to curse him or call him a shithead. Wanda grew up with the impression that her mother mostly felt sorry for him. Wanda has four memories of her father and now that she is reaching thirty, they are blurrier around the edges. She remembers his long hair and his square oversized glasses; she is reminded of him when she sees hipster graduate students at UF show up for orientation. He is gangly, tall. She dreams that he is a bendy straw and that she, a giant, uses him to suck up seawater. She asks her therapist what they think that means and they say, "He is hollow inside, but you make him useful." Wanda nods, solemnly.

"I have a question, Wanda," her therapist adds. "In your dream, were you swimming or were you drowning?"

When she feels comfortable enough to share, Wanda tells the group how she figured it out. "My father left when I was eight, ran away like a little boy with only a scribbled note on the back of a receipt for cereal and toilet paper. It said something about it being better for me, that he wasn't meant to be a father, that it would hurt me and my mother more if he stayed.

"And that was that. My mom and I, we got closer. It was the two of us versus everything. Then one day, when I was sixteen, I found a hairbrush of his in the back of her closet and I kept it until I was twenty. I sent strands of his hair to a lab I found on the internet, along with a tube of my spit.

"Maybe if he wasn't actually my father, I could forgive him for leaving. And while my mother had never mentioned a lover, she'd alluded that things were complicated, gave me reason to believe that something had happened. Or maybe it was the opposite, and I was searching for a concrete, biological, bodily connection to him, even if it lived only on a piece of paper. What does it matter now? When the results came back, it said that while we were related, he was not my father—probably, instead, an uncle. When I confronted my mother, she looked baffled, said it was impossible. She screamed at me for maybe the first time in my whole life; she asked why I would play such a cruel joke on her. Her face was contorted and ugly. 'Do you think your mother is some kind of liar?' she asked. She raised her hand up, but never brought it down on my body."

Wanda stops telling her story abruptly. She feels tightness in her cheeks and does not want to cry in front of her computer screen and the people in the tiny boxes on it. Some of the people in the tiny boxes nod, and Phillip puts a heart next to his face in his box. Wanda interprets this as understanding. There are a few additional affirmations in the chat, and Wanda sends a < and a 3 as a thank you. And then the next person starts sharing, talks about her own uncle-father and the individual sadness and hurt that relationship has wrought.

When she logs off, she searches for her partner, who is in the living room watching a television show about white people surviving in the wilderness. Their cat, mostly black with a single white spot beneath his nose that looks like a mustache, sits on her lap, basking in both the heat from her crotch as well as the rays of sun coming through the window.

"How was it?" Grace asks Wanda. She pauses the show on the image of a man skinning a porcupine he caught by clubbing it with a tree branch.

Wanda shrugs. She has been with Grace coming on three years, met her through friends of friends, a little web of dykes who were sometimes born in and sometimes drawn to Gainesville for one reason or another. Grace had spontaneously moved to Jacksonville after meeting a group of queers through some random straight guy she had met on the internet and then had eventually moseyed down the seventy-two miles southwest to the even smaller Florida city. When drunk, Grace likes to talk about ghosts, about the experience of being haunted. When she's even drunker, she leans in close to whoever is nearest and whispers, "But do you think you could fuck a ghost?" Wanda forgives her for these moments of vulgarity. In fact, it is Grace's openness that draws her in close. Sharing seems to come so easy to Grace: first her home and her cat, and then, as cheesy as it sounds, her heart. Wanda stays shut like a sand-filled clam.

"Okay, my love," Grace says. "Tell me about it when you're ready, if you want to."

Wanda wants to. She remembers when she had first met Grace—how they, in their first conversation, joked about their

ACE scores. Wanda had learned about Adverse Childhood Experiences in a social work class she had taken as an undergrad, Grace from being an advocate at the rape crisis center. They lamented that the original framework didn't account for racism, for homophobia, for transphobia, for so many of the things that shaped their lives.

"So, I get one point for my parents' divorce, but there is nothing in here about your father actually being your uncle," Wanda had said, in the hazy light of the bar. The half-empty beer in her hand made her feel brave and silly. Grace looked at her, wide-eyed.

"I'm sorry? What did you just say?" she asked. She put her hand around her ear like a cone, goofy.

"The man I thought was my father, was actually my uncle." Wanda explained, giggling, her voice like a slushy in her mouth. "But! It's not because my mom slept with brothers—" And the whole story tumbled out amid her girlish and flirty laughs.

Wanda lies down in Grace's lap. Her head nestles in between Grace's soft belly and their cat's body. She can feel Grace's breath moving through her body and the vibration of the cat's purrs. *There are bees in there*, she thinks to herself in Grace's voice, an inside joke between the two of them.

"I think it's my fault," she says finally, more into Grace's shirt than at her. Grace says nothing, instead runs her fingers through Wanda's hair. Wanda falls asleep, her scalp tingling.

Her mother's garden is lush. Squash on arched trellises, above-ground garden boxes full of kale, red lettuce, arugula, and bok choy. Large circular planters grow tomatoes, and circular tree stumps create winding paths between fruits, vegetables, flowers, and herbs. Wanda thinks about the conversation she recently had with Grace about how, botanically speaking, fruit is a use-less category. Wanda told her that was homophobic.

"Mom?" Wanda opens the back door to her mother's house, the house she had mostly been raised in. It is now shared with Wanda's stepdad, Bill, but Wanda likes to time her visits for when she knows Bill isn't home. There's nothing wrong with him; when Wanda is out of his presence, she can admit that he is kind and generous, that he treats her mother well.

"In here," her mother calls from the room that was once Wanda's but is now filled with sewing materials, books, and art projects. Her mother's peppered hair is still long, now almost past her lower back. She has a headlamp stretched around her forehead, a pair of pliers in her hand.

"Can you turn that off?" Wanda asks when her mother looks up at her, the light shining in her eyes.

"Sorry," her mother says. The word is stiff in her mouth. "How's it going? What's going on?"

"Nothing," Wanda says. "I just wanted to come by and say hi."

"Okay," her mother says. "Hi." She smiles at her daughter while ushering her out to the kitchen.

Wanda's mother brings her a plate of cut peaches and a glass of sparkling orange juice. Everything is sweet and sticky in her mouth and on her hands and Wanda feels like a child again, just home from school on a warm afternoon.

"How is work? Grace?" she asks. Wanda's mouth is full but she nods as if to say, *Fine, everything is fine.*

"Grace got that promotion," Wanda tells her once she has swallowed.

"Good for her. I'll send her a card or a gift to say congratulations. What do you think she'd like?"

"She doesn't need anything, Mom."

"Why does it have to be something she needs?" her mother looks at her incredulously. *Are you even my daughter?* Wanda sees this in the question marks strewn across her face, knitted into her eyebrows.

"A plant would be nice," Wanda concedes. "Maybe a clipping from your garden in one of the pots you've been throwing."

Her mother's kitchen table sits right underneath the largest window in the house, one that looks out over the expansive and tidy, but wild, garden. Wanda sees her mom smile at the suggestion, watches her look out the window to shop for the perfect one, momentarily.

"Mom?" A pause. "Mom?"

"What?"

"I want to talk about Daddy," she says quietly. She doesn't know why she says "Daddy." It feels right in that moment, maybe a way to get her mother to see her like a child again.

Her mother doesn't look at Wanda, keeps her eyes out at the window. A bird lands on one of her feeders, the one that she greased with kitchen oil to keep squirrels from climbing up the pole to steal the mixture of seeds.

"Mom." Her voice is something resembling stern, as close to stern as she can get.

"What about him? It's been over twenty years, Wanda." Her mother asks without looking confused.

"And here I am," Wanda says, with a shrug and tears in her eyes. "Twenty years later." She knows better than to cry in front of her mother, but her loneliness, her emptiness, her shame bubbles up from her stomach, into her chest, up through her throat and out of her eyes. They are big, fat, salty tears.

"It's not my fault," Wanda says, "that Daddy"—there's that word again—"left. And it's not my fault that he didn't tell you what was going on. And it's not my fault for figuring it out." Wanda doesn't believe any of this, really. But she says it to convince her mother and herself.

"That's correct," her mother says. Wanda wishes she had the type of mother who would reach toward her, lean forward, and grab her hand. She thinks she remembers that her mother once was that type.

"Then why are you still so mad at me? Why can't we talk about it?"

"I don't know," her mother admits.

"I feel like—" Wanda struggles for the words. "I feel like big pieces of me are missing. I can feel it—" she starts to grab parts of herself with her hands. "In my body, Mom. As if parts of my bones are hollow or muscle mass is gone and can never come back."

"Like you are part ghost," her mother says, clear like an echo.

"Yes," Wanda says. And then she wonders, is this what it feels like to be understood by my mother? It does not feel as good as she had anticipated. Instead, the dread in her body grows like a fungus; the dread in her body is alive.

"Like you are the reaper and the reaped," Wanda's mother continues. "I have heard these things before, Wanda. I—"

Wanda interrupts. "Remember when I got the test results back and I brought them to you?" she asks.

Wanda's mother nods slowly.

"I always thought you were mad because I questioned your honor or something. Or because I implied you were a liar. But—" she falters for a second. "I get it now."

Wanda returns home with a small monstera plant in a blue clay pot. Around the lip of the pot her mother tied a ribbon with a small card that simply says, *Grace*.

"How was it, babe?" Grace asks when she hears the front door open and then close.

"I think she hates me," Wanda says.

"Your mom does not hate you," Grace responds, a reflex.

"She's scared of me."

"She's not scared of you."

"Grace."

"What, baby?" Grace looks at her, frustrated, and Wanda knows that this is a lot, that she is a lot. She can feel herself exceeding the limits of Grace's patience, the dough of her body rising beyond its container.

"You don't know," she says.

"I don't know what? What it's like to be estranged from my parents?" Grace's face hardens. She takes the plant from Wanda's hands and looks around the room. "My mother would never give you a plant, that's for sure. I don't even know if she can keep anything alive."

"You're alive."

"Despite her."

Grace picks a sunny spot for the monstera, moves another to make room for it. She gives it a drink. Wanda thinks about Grace's mother, a cold woman who refuses to speak to her daughter, hasn't seen her in five years, and then she looks at Grace, so different, both absorbing and reflecting the sunshine as it enters their home. Wanda stays seated on their couch, focuses on the pilling of the cushions instead of her partner. She plucks the pieces of lint between her fingers, collects them into a growing ball in her palm. She plucks and thinks about inheritance, plucks and thinks about what we give and what we keep.

"You know, I think the only way you'll be like him is if you let your life be ruined by this thing," Grace says, finally. And then she walks out of the room because there is nothing else for her to say.

"Well, that felt a little on the nose," Wanda says, cracking a smile, but she has only the plants as her companions. She drops her lint ball on the floor, pushes it underneath the couch with her foot. Sheepishly, she shuffles into the next room to find Grace again. She goes up to her, wraps her arms around her waist, pulls her in and soaks her up.

FUTURE: DEATH

Grieve, transform, end.

She will find him when he is living in a retirement home in South Florida. He never made it out of the sunshine state after all. He will be easy to find, so easy it will make Wanda feel stupid for not looking sooner.

Grace, while no longer Wanda's lover, will live in a house down the street with a wife and two dogs. They will have weekly dinners on Sundays. Her mother will be dead for, wow, has it been five years already? Wanda will have the occasional sweetheart, but nothing permanent. She will always have a job, but not one for very long. Bill will live in her mother's house and tend to her mother's garden, but Wanda will never see it again after her mother's funeral, will not even drive by. Her mother will leave her a little bit of money that will allow her to buy her own house, though she will never have any luck growing things in its yard.

Wanda will drive down to South Florida three times, all with the intention to—to see? to watch? to look at? him. She will not be sure until the fourth time, when she will park her car in front of the building, get out of the car, and go to the front desk. She will ask to see Arthur Zhao, and when asked who she is, she will be truthful, will say, "His daughter, Wanda," and slide her ID across the counter. It will be easier than she expected—there will not be a lot of security and he will not have told the staff to bar his daughter from visiting. Why would he?

She will find him in a common room, other visitors laughing or talking quietly with their loved ones. The room will be described as sun-drenched. It will be a nice place. She will wonder how he could afford it.

In the five years after her mother's death, Wanda will have found forgiveness for both of her parents. She will have found her own ways to assuage the empty, ghostlike parts of herself. She will not meet her father with scorn or resentment. All she will have is curiosity.

Wanda will walk up behind him, will fight the childish impulse to sneak up on him, to frighten him, to whisper *boo*. She will remember that there is no precedent in their relationship for that kind of game. She will be a forty-year-old woman, not an eight-year-old girl.

Instead she will softly, kindly, touch his shoulder. She will be next to him so he can see her shape in his periphery.

She will say, "Daddy? It's me. I'm here."

Migratory Patterns

It was the most recent goodbye party in a series of six good-bye parties over the past two years. Lou and their girlfriend had moved to Seattle, Melissa to Richmond. Others had moved to Chicago and Durham, to Baltimore and Amsterdam. And Rebecca, well, she had been gone for years, though they all kept a space carved out of their gatherings and their bodies for her. The crowd was small—the leftovers, they sometimes joked with each other—but music could still be heard coming from Danny's backyard, a group of people sitting in plastic Adirondack chairs placed in a circle on the cement patio under the carport.

It was a hot one, not surprising for July in Jacksonville. Citronella candles were lit, and everyone smelled like sunscreen, bug spray, and sweat. A plastic kiddie pool had recently been filled from a nearby hose. Toys from the dollar store floated on the surface: frogs, ducks, a flamingo. Lizards rustled in the grass, hand-held fans whooshed the air around them.

The side gate opened, and a tall, lanky queer in a knit crop top and cut-off shorts walked through with a twirl.

149

"Hey, babies," Taylor said in a singsong as they touched Rachel's shoulder. She turned her head and smiled at them, rubbed their stubbly cheek with the back of her hand.

"Hi, T."

The rest of the group waved sweetly to Taylor and then to Justin, who was not far behind, sunglasses on top of his head, newly shaved in preparation for the summer heat.

Rachel was moving to Atlanta for nursing school, but mostly to just get the hell out for a while. "Maybe I'll finally date a queer who hasn't fucked one of my friends," she'd been joking with anyone who asked. None of her friends had the heart to tell her that even in a city as big as Atlanta, the incestuousness of queer dating would follow her like a persistent cough.

"How's packing going?" Justin asked her.

"Fine, fine." Rachel said, with a wave of her hand. "It's practically done."

Danny, her roommate, scoffed next to the grill they were in charge of. From the backyard you couldn't see the still-flat boxes leaning in the hallway, the piles of clothes on the floor. The bathroom, somewhat dingy, had been left untouched.

"What?" Rachel whined.

"I didn't say anything," they said.

"You did."

"Surprise!" Everyone turned to the voice at the gate.

"Ashley?"

The whole group exclaimed, got up at once, and ran toward their friend, who could barely pass the threshold, too many arms enveloping her. "You're already here?" "When did you get in?" "Oh my god, honey!" "Why didn't you tell me you were here? I would have scooped you." Only Danny stayed behind, at their post behind the grill, though they could still see the glitter applied around her eyes, the red lipstick on her mouth, her wide and bright smile as she was hugged and squeezed by their friends. When she had departed two years before, they hadn't expected her to make her way back, so quickly, like a beautiful and intoxicating boomerang.

"Hey, friend," she said quietly. Suddenly, she was next to them.

"Hi, Ashley," they replied, opening one of their arms to her, inviting her into a side hug while keeping their eyes on the food in front of them.

She fit snugly, comfortably, against their chest, their belly— their bodies remembering how to embrace each other.

"I missed you," she said, breathing the smell of them in, the smoke from the charcoal grill making sense of her memories of them.

"I missed you too."

The party continued, with hot dogs, coleslaw, potato and maca- roni salads, a thick and saccharine banana pudding, saran wrap wadded up on the table, hands swatting flies and mosquitoes away, Bluetooth speakers pushing out music by sad girls and the occasional upbeat dance hit, until someone's phone started dying and so another person connected theirs and a different playlist was chosen.

Danny sat in the sun, away from the others, their eyes closed. They soaked in the heat, the music, the voices and laughter of their friends—sometimes rising to a crescendo and other times just barely audible over the music.

"You doing okay?" Taylor asked Danny, sitting down on their lap and running their hand through their brown curls.

"Yeah, of course," Danny said, their voice dreamy and warm from the IPAs, chilled in the cooler and then sweating in their hand.

"You sure?"

"Why are you asking?" Danny replied.

"By the look on your face, you weren't expecting Ashley to come over."

"I thought it might be a possibility, but you know Ashley. It's hard to pin her down."

"Mmhm."

"I'm happy she's back," Danny said. "It's nice to have someone come home for once."

"So true," Taylor sighed, looking over at their partner Justin. "Especially since I don't think I'm going anywhere for a while."

"Justin never talks about wanting to leave?" Danny asked.

"No, his whole family is here, his job, the drag show," they said. "Besides, this is home. I wouldn't know where to go even if it was an option. Anyway, Ashley—"

"Yes?"

"I heard she broke up with her girlfriend in Chicago."

"You heard?"

"She told me. We caught up on the phone during her drive down."

Danny shrugged, tried to hide their embarrassment. It had been years ago, their mostly small crush that sometimes swelled into something bigger and harder to hold on to. There was that one summer, their one birthday that they thought something might happen, but Ashley and Melissa had just broken up and then Rebecca died and it had all felt like jumping into the coldest, clearest water—shock, relief, and then just too much.

They ran their finger over the seams on Taylor's tank top. Danny and Taylor had met in college, had traveled across the country with each other, had written postcards when, for a few years, Taylor had lived in Budapest and then Portland, Maine. As baby gays they would wrestle after too many shots, always the first to exclaim in amusement and the last to leave a party or a bar. Danny had almost moved to Portland to join Taylor, when their missing of them and their need for a break in the humidity had both reached a peak. Danny was very good at almost.

Either way, Taylor came back after a few years, met Justin, settled into a small house only two blocks away with a large porch now covered in potted plants.

"I think you need to make a move," Taylor said.

"What are you talking about?"

"Say something, do something."

Danny wiggled their almost empty beer, heard the remaining drink and spit swish in the glass. Taylor's weight started to hurt their thighs, they adjusted, but Taylor remained.

"Ever since Rebecca—" Taylor started.

"I don't want to talk about Rebecca," Danny said. "For once, can we all be around each other and it not revolve around Rebecca?"

"Maybe?"

Danny chortled at them, an annoyed, gruff-sounding noise from their throat.

"Maybe we could if you would *do something*. Ever since she died, you've just been here, and if Max hadn't gotten that job in Austin you probably would still be living in her fucking house with him. We're what, three blocks away from it?"

Danny shrugged Taylor off roughly, stood up. Taylor's voice had been raised, but the music was loud enough that nobody paid them any attention.

"Someone had to say it," Taylor said. "Rebecca would have said it."

"This is stupid," they said, finally.

"Yes, you are stupid," Taylor told them. "But I love you." They pulled Danny into their chest, rested their cheek on top of Danny's curls. Danny's eyes started to mist, but Taylor couldn't see it because Danny's face was tucked so tightly into their chest. And they stayed like that, until another friend wandered over, hugged them both tightly without knowing the context.

Ashley sat next to Rachel on the bench nearest to the fire. They had never been close, mostly just orbiting each other and their shared beloveds, but Ashley was still sad to see her go, and Rachel was disappointed that Ashley had moved back just as she was leaving. There was potential for something deeper and they both knew it, and that created a hypothetical nostalgia that hugged them both close.

"You don't think you'll miss Chicago?" Rachel asked Ashley.

"No, it wasn't for me." Ashley said. "And it was stupid of me to move for another person. Who knew that a lesbian U-Haul might not actually be the best strategy for long-term, healthy partnership?"

"We've all been there. Remember the six months I spent in Austin with whatever-her-name-was?"

"Leslie."

"Ugh, what a mistake." Leslie was a soccer dyke with a large and encompassing temper that had scared Rachel and her friends.

They gave each other a side squeeze, tears welling up in Rachel's eyes, not the first or last time that night. It was in moments like this that she felt the worst about leaving. How long would it take her to build friendships like these? It would be months before she'd have a grocery store that felt comfortable in Atlanta, maybe a decade before she could have the intimacy of real friendship.

"How's your dad doing?" Rachel asked. She had heard that he was really the reason Ashley had returned, that her father's cancer had come back, that her siblings were overwhelmed and Ashley, being the most grounded of them all, had been called home.

"He's fine," Ashley said, her voice tight. "Everyone's happy that I'm back, that's for sure."

Rachel reached for Ashley's hand. Ashley, not one to show her emotions, looked crumpled, her shoulders rolled forward and her eyes damp, if not wet.

"I'm tired," Ashley said. "And I'm trying not to resent—being back. I don't hate it here, by any means, and I'm so happy to have queer family here. I just—" She took a deep, raspy breath in. "I just wasn't ready, I think."

"That makes sense," Rachel said, feeling a growing sense of something like survivor's guilt. "Will you come visit me in Atlanta? When you need to get away."

Ashley laughed, leaned her head into Rachel's shoulder. "Yes," she said. "I'd really love that."

Justin felt suffocated by the moisture in the air, the bonfire, the feelings of his friends. He went inside and sat at the small table in Danny's kitchen, his back to the air conditioning vent. Danny's and Rachel's plants were dying—sad succulents had gone squishy and limp; ferns had shriveled up, only a step away from dust. On his phone, Justin knew, there was an email with a job offer in North Carolina. The pay was better, there would be opportunities to grow. He was sure he could relaunch the show, *Fish Camp*, in Durham, and he could more easily travel up north to Philly, DC, and New York. He took his phone out and opened the email again. *We're so pleased to offer you . . .* , he read for the sixth, and then seventh, time. Justin hopped onto his Zillow and Trulia apps. How much would a one-bedroom cost? Maybe there was a queer housing Facebook group he could join; roommates would be nice, a built-in social life for at least a few months could cushion the blow. Maybe he'd get a cat, which he hadn't done in Florida because Taylor said they were allergic.

Guilt rushed down his torso, spread into his arms and then legs. *Fuck.* There had been a few times he had tried to broach the subject of breaking up, or at least he thought he had. T was like a slippery eel in his hands, and he couldn't hold them long enough to tell them. It was their fault, he reasoned, that he hadn't told them about applying for jobs out of state. *Besides,* he thought, *it's not like I'm cheating on them.* In Justin's mind, there were always worse types of deception that made his own feel more forgivable.

Ashley stepped into the kitchen, sat across from him with a tight smile.

"I haven't seen you all night," she said.

"It's hot," Justin said with a playful whine, pouting his lips for effect.

"Yeah, okay." Ashley said, suspicion in every syllable. She narrowed her eyes at him, placed her forearms on the sticky table. She had forgotten about this kitchen table, how it was covered in a vinyl that always felt tacky. She hadn't been gone long, just over a year, but now that she was being confronted by things she had so easily forgotten, she felt a backlog of something like homesickness.

"How does it feel to be back?" Justin asked her.

"I don't know, I just got here," Ashley said snappily. Now Justin was the one to narrow his eyes at her, look more closely and deliberately at his friend.

"Yeah, okay," he mocked her. Ashley went to kick him underneath the table but missed his shins and found an iron table leg instead. "Ow!"

"Serves you right, bitch," Justin said with a giggle. Ashley laughed too, tried not to wince as her big toe throbbed.

"When's the next *Fish Camp*? I saw last month's was *Survivor* themed. I'm sad I couldn't be there."

"Yeah, it was fun to see what all the girls could do with a buff and a Jeff Probst sound clip. I'm not sure if everyone got the references, though."

"What's next?"

"I don't know," he sighed. "I'm feeling uninspired."

Ashley's face remained mostly unchanged but she didn't break eye contact with him. Justin knew he was being a brat, saw it reflected in his friend's face. He wasn't going to tell her about the job even if he felt like yelling the news to her, to someone, to anyone.

"What's going on with Justin?" Rachel asked Taylor. The speaker's battery had died, so they were instead being serenaded by the cicadas. Rachel had been watching Justin sulk through the kitchen window for most of the evening. Now that it was dark, the glow of his phone, which he kept putting into his pocket and then taking out again, lit up his frowning face.

"Who knows," Taylor said. They grabbed a kielbasa from the grill and smothered it with mustard and kraut. It seemed like the couple had been avoiding each other the whole party—Justin had come out for food and a short chat with Danny before retreating back into the house. And while he giggled with anyone who sat across from him and petted Lucy, Danny's old lab who lay at his feet, he hadn't wrapped his arm around Taylor's waist like he would usually, wasn't fanning himself in an Adirondack chair, unbothered by the mosquitoes.

And Taylor, they were just as clearly annoyed. They flitted from one friend to another but kept an eye on their partner inside. "He's being rude," they told Rachel, before stuffing the sausage in their mouth. And then, with their mouth full, added, "A real asshole."

Rachel's eyebrows knitted in concern. "Y'all okay?"

Taylor and Justin were one of the couples that felt like family to her, her two friends who would host dinner parties and big holidays like Christmas, when friends couldn't or didn't want to go home.

"Fine," Taylor said. Justin's aloofness wasn't new, but it was something Taylor had learned to navigate. Taylor was invested: in Justin, the home they shared, they life they were building. They would chide Justin later, tell him how it had hurt their feelings. They would make up before going to bed and things would keep moving in the direction Taylor had been directing them toward.

Rachel looked unconvinced, had been noticing more and more moments of tension between her friends. She pushed a little, said, "It would be okay, if y'all weren't fine."

Taylor shot her a look of annoyance. "I know that," they said.

"Okay," Rachel replied. "I'm just saying."

"Saying what?"

Rachel had picked at a scab that Taylor didn't like to acknowledge was there.

"That relationships are complicated, and it would be completely understandable if shit was hard right now."

"I don't need a therapist, Rachel," Taylor said. Their voice was snotty; they could hear it, dripping out of their own mouth, running away from them before they could catch it. They weren't trying to figure out what it would mean if things didn't work out with Justin, especially as they were about to say goodbye to one of their best friends. You can only say so many goodbyes before you start to get bitter and resentful.

"Sorry," they said after a few moments of silence.

"It's okay, baby," Rachel said. "It's a lot." She patted their arm and felt that feeling again, that twinge of guilt.

And then they were all together around the fire. Ashley sat next to Danny, who sat next to Taylor, who sat next to Rachel, who sat next to Justin, who sat on Ashley's other side. Danny had switched to water once Rachel handed them a glass jar with a quip that they weren't twenty-five anymore. They had been thinking of doing a month of sobriety for six months, but the beginnings and then middles of months always seemed to race by so quickly. Still, they didn't want to be hungover the next day when Rachel inevitably asked them to help her finish packing.

They could feel Ashley next to them, even though they weren't touching. Could feel their presence on their whole right side: from their cheek to their shoulder to their belly to their thigh down to their ankle. An invisible pressure pressing against them, uncomfortable and hot—though maybe that was because of the fire.

She turned to them, caught their eye. "Haven't seen you very much tonight," she said.

"A host's job is never done," they joked. Danny had been keeping busy cleaning up and putting plates and platters in a pile in the sink, tossing empties and almost empties into the recycling can. Normally, they wouldn't have bothered, but it was hard to feel cheery as they grieved the loss of Rachel and spiraled about Ashley's return.

Ashley nodded, a little solemn. "Did I—do something? We haven't talked—"

"No, no, of course not," Danny said, quickly.

"Oh," Ashley responded. "Okay."

"I'm sorry," Danny said. "I don't know why I'm nervous."

"Nervous?"

"Or anxious. Something—"

"About me?" Ashley's heartbeat quickened, and her face felt hot—or was that fire? She chastised herself for not reaching out to Danny earlier; she should have called them before she arrived, she shouldn't have just shown up to the party.

"I love that you're back," Danny tried to backtrack, to reassure her. "It's just complicated—"

Ashley nodded. That, she could agree with. It had always been complicated. And while she never regretted the one night they let things get muddled, she still dismissed her bubbling feelings for her good friend as a spell the springs had cast on them.

Still, she wanted to be honest with them. "You're the only reason moving back isn't horrible," she said. She could feel the stinging tears gathering at the corners of her eyes. "My family is a mess, and the idea of taking care of my dad, with all of our past shit, terrifies me." Danny put their hand on Ashley's arm. Ashley continued, "But knowing that you'd be here made it feel possible."

The buzz of their friends' conversations stopped, suddenly dead. Ashley and Danny could both feel them all looking at them. They turned away from each other. Rachel, the person directly across from them, looked at them with concern. Nobody asked if they were okay, but they watched both Ashley and Danny wipe tears away from their eyes.

"I know, I know," Rachel said, coming to their rescue. "Everybody is going to miss me so much."

"We are, bitch," Danny said with a deep laugh. "We are."

"Justin and I are already planning our visit," Taylor added.

"We are?" Justin asked, dry. It felt like a balloon was being blown up in his chest. He could picture Taylor's look of annoyance without even looking at them, but it didn't stop him. "Guess I've got to do what Daddy tells me." They punctuated their sentence with an eye roll.

Rachel pushed his arm, gently but with a little bite. "Stop," she said under her breath.

"What's your problem tonight?" Taylor asked.

"I'm just joking. It's fine," Justin replied.

"You're being an asshole," Taylor snapped back.

"I'm really not," Justin said. "But if that's the picture you want to create for your friends, then that's fine. I can be the bad guy."

"We're not just *their* friends," Danny said.

"Okay," Justin said with a scoff.

"Are you serious?" Danny asked. "We've been friends for years."

"Yeah, well, that's nothing compared to over a decade," Justin responded, shooting a look at Taylor.

"Let's go inside, Justin," Ashley said. She started to get up.

"No, I'm good," Justin said. "I'm going to walk home."

"Without me?" Taylor asked.

"Yes," Justin said. He turned around quickly, adding, "I'll text you before you leave, Rachel." He didn't say anything to anyone else.

"What the hell was that?" Danny asked. They looked over at Taylor, whose head was in their hands.

"I don't know," Rachel said, standing up next to them now. "Let's give him some space." She patted Taylor's back and started to herd them inside.

"Maybe they can help you pack," Danny joked to Rachel. She shot them a dirty look as she walked inside.

"Has it been like this?" Ashley asked. And Danny tried to remember any other signs of discontent; they felt bad for not remembering, for maybe not noticing.

"I don't know," they responded truthfully. "But I'm sure they'll be fine."

They had been here before—alone after a long night with friends, a web of anticipation and uncertainty spun between them. But it had been years, and they were older and held new and heavier pockets of disappointment and grief and yearning than before. Ashley leaned her body close to Danny, her head resting on their shoulder.

"Do you remember my birthday? The one before Rebecca died?" Danny asked her.

"Of course," Ashley said. "One of the last great trips."

"There was that moment—" Danny sat up a little straighter, squarely looked at Ashley's face. "I wanted to kiss you."

"I wanted you to kiss me," Ashley said. And then, "So why didn't you?"

"You, Melissa, Lou. I don't know. It felt like too much," they said.

Ashley looked down at that, nodded.

"Or, maybe, I don't know, if I'm being honest—" they started.

She looked up at them, her face open and bright, again, like the fucking moon.

"I was scared," they admitted. "But I don't want to be scared anymore."

"I don't want you to be scared either," she affirmed.

So, they reached down, cupped her cheek in their hand and lifted it toward their face. She leaned in, mimicked her hand on their face—and they met in the middle, their lips and then their tongues touching. And it felt like—

It felt like coming home.

A Packing List for the
End of the World

FIRST AID KIT: When I was in elementary school in California, there were earthquake kits and drills that taught us to huddle beneath our tiny desks to protect ourselves from the falling rubble and debris—only a small sheet of wood to shield our small bodies from a crumbling ceiling and everything else that was toppling beyond it. Later, in Florida, there were hurricane kits. During a lonely year in Kansas, a tornado kit. Always preparing for a different disaster.

TENT: We have one from Target that fits us, our blow-up mattress, and Biscuit, snuggly but comfortably. It was only $29.99. A real deal. We probably can't bring the blow-up mattress, though. It's too heavy, and eventually we'll run out of batteries for the pump. I'm assuming batteries are going to be hard to come by. That sucks because Ty has chronic back pain. That's something you don't see on *The Walking Dead*—herniated discs.

WATER: I don't know how many times I've googled, *Does seltzer hydrate you the same as regular water?* Results are inconclusive.

BOOTS: It just seems like the most practical shoe choice. As a queer who has lived in the South, I have many pairs to choose from, though it's tricky because my favorite pair technically belongs to Ty. We both wear a size 7. I bought them as a Christmas gift for Ty a few years back. They'll probably want to wear them. I wonder how much longer Zappos will deliver.

PICTURES: When my Gung Gung died, we spent a whole night looking through old pictures, government documents, newspaper clippings. It was soon to be my uncle's house and I was struck by how I still called it my Popo's house, even though she had died over ten years before. My uncle made me promise that I wouldn't take anything important because he wanted to keep the family history together. I slipped photos of my great-grandparents, my Gung Gung's parents, into my backpack, instead of allowing them to be forgotten in an unorganized box in the back of my dead Popo's closet. I've never been very obedient. My great-grandparents stare blankly at the camera, the photograph cropped at their chests. They are the only photos I've ever seen of them. I kept them because I do not know how to pronounce their names.

BOBBY PINS: I'll lose them all in the first week. They'll keep the hair out of my face until then.

~~THE CATS~~: We have this debate almost every day. I just don't believe cats are that domesticated. Oscar and Cleo will be better off without us than with us. Biscuit lives up to his name, a soft and loyal dog who cries with stuffed toys he holds in his mouth every time we leave the house. Ty is going to say that I only think this because I don't like cats, that I favor Biscuit, but that's not true. The cats have really grown on me.

STRAP-ON: My friend once told me about driving across the Canadian border with their partner. They had a bag full of sex toys in their trunk. When the Canadian border agents went through it, they opened the bag and became so embarrassed by the sex toys they just let my friends go through. I'd like to think that people still fuck in the apocalypse, that we'll still fuck in the apocalypse. It could feel urgent and good. We won't have to fear accidentally repopulating a dying planet.

MATCHES: I was never good at lighting fires, too timid around them. Never a Girl Scout, not even a Brownie.

SOCKS + UNDERWEAR: Days-of-the-week underwear were a practical invention. I don't think they make them anymore, so I took a black Sharpie and wrote Monday through Sunday on the back of seven plain white pairs. Tuesday was written in bubble letters, Wednesday in a delicate cursive for hump day. It will help me keep time. When it all ends for good, I'll want to know if it's a Thursday.

CLOTHES: Not all the shirts can be crop tops.

KNIFE: What is it like, ripping and tearing into flesh? Does each puncture feel like a loss, or like a gain? Will I be able to do it if the person looks like my mom, or my cousin, or the person who used to work at the movie theater and always gave me a student-priced ticket even though I was twenty-seven and had been rejected from every graduate program I applied to? If our survival is always at the expense of someone or something else, is it even worth it?

ANTIDOTE: There isn't one.

BUG SPRAY: In the summer, I play connect-the-dots with the bug bites on my legs. With a ballpoint pen, my bites become whales, water bursting through their blowholes, forests of coral, the ocean floor. As the days—no, hours—go on, the bites start to swell. The whales balloon into unidentifiable blobs and the waves of the ocean expand. I'm not supposed to itch, so I resort to slapping at the bites, scratching circles around their perimeters.

SNACKS: I had moved out to Florida only four years before. That summer, Ty flew out to California and helped me pack up my car; we drove to the Grand Canyon and then down south and then east. In a gas station in small-town Texas, I remember calling them by their name. I never call them by their name, but in that aisle full of pickle-flavored chips and sunflower seeds, glass cases of Cheerwine—my favorite—there was an almost unnoticed beat, a brief breath where I chose to not call them *baby*. Because I love them, I called them by their name in that gas station in small-town Texas—because we are small, and the world is big, and everything is bigger in Texas. I kept my hands in my back pocket so mine didn't reach for theirs. I wanted to tangle fingers in their hair, draw shapes on their back. My hands wanted to call them *baby*. And even with my hands restrained and their name on my tongue, I could still feel the eyes of the men behind the counter on my skin. Because I think they could see my whole body call Ty *baby*, and their whole body respond *yes*.

ROPE: One website had lists for small disasters and what they called "Armageddon." The man—I'm assuming it was a man because masculinity asserts itself in the most obnoxious ways—suggested multiple types of rope for various purposes. He also suggested a knot-tying guide to help tie the rope for these various purposes. I went to Home Depot, a common ground for dykes and bigots alike, and bought the suggested rope. I also bought some houseplants, because they were having an end-of-the-world sale and I couldn't leave all of them there to die; some Clorox wipes, because we had run out a few weeks before and I used them to clean our bathroom sink; a pack of gum; and a Coke, even though I had stopped drinking soda for health reasons. What did it matter now? The line was long, wrapping itself around the store like a well-behaved and dying snake. My arms ached from the fullness of my purchases by the time I reached the washers and dryers, so I rested the rope on a washing machine for just a moment. When I finally reached checkout, I only had one small succulent and the Coke in my hands. I paid for them—$5.99, after tax. It was only a few days later, after we abandoned our small brick house, that I remembered the rope— similarly abandoned on top of the washing machine. Now we would have to find something else to make traps or climb things or give up completely, because sometimes your body can only take so much.

PILLOW, ONE FOR EACH OF US: We are both convinced that the other is a blanket hog. Each of us wakes up in the middle of the night playing a silent and sleepy game of tug-o-war. When we moved in together, they claimed my favorite pillow, one that is so squishy that it fills itself between your arms and your face. After a few months, I tried to take it back. *It's mine*, I said. But they pouted and insisted that it was theirs now, that they were bonded with the pillow. I relented. Now, when I pack up our car, I pick that pillow for them and another one for me.

PLANT: We made space for the succulent on the dashboard of our car and when the sun hits it on our endless drives you can see it reach toward its rays. I've never been good at keeping plants alive, but this one feels more urgent. Biscuit wraps himself into a tight cinnamon roll in the back seat, and Ty's eyes drift sweetly to me in forgetful moments. It almost feels like we're driving through Texas again, though the roads are mostly abandoned and there's nothing to put on the radio. It's in these moments that I force myself to remember that the car will run out of gas eventually, that I don't know how much I can carry on my back. It's heavy, this doubt and fear. Even the loss feels heavy, as it carves out a space for itself inside each of my muscles; I can feel it in every move my body makes. I decide to put the plant in the ground the next time we stop, to insist that something I've loved will survive me.

FLASHLIGHT: The layers of darkness are what get to me, the way that it closes around you as the sun sets, the movement from light blue to orange to pink and then purple, then navy, dark like velvet, then finally black. Biscuit doesn't like sleeping in the tent because he is also afraid of the dark. When we used to go camping, the tips of his ears would stay alert as he listened to the life rustling in the bushes. Before, it was usually armadillos, wild pigs, and other critters. I'm not sure what Biscuit makes of undead rustling, of slightly dead rustling, of nonpeople who used to be people making their way through the forest as we huddle in our tent, holding our breath.

Acknowledgments

For me, writing has never been a solitary act, but one always done with and among others. I am humbled by all the care and support I have received over the almost ten years I have been working on these stories and am honored to have the opportunity to name a few of those people, communities, and organizations here—

My agent, Soumeya Bendimerad Roberts, who believed in me and these stories even when my own faith faltered. How grateful I am for your steadiness and brilliance. Hannah Popal and the rest of the HG Literary team.

My wonderful editor, Marisa Siegel. Everyone at Northwestern University Press who so thoughtfully stewarded this book out into the world and readers' hands: Beth Blachman, Morgan Krehbiel, Maia Rigas, Madeline Schultz, Kristen Twardowski, and others.

My teachers—Victor Bascara, Lucy M. Burns, Keith Camacho, M. Evelina Galang, Lydia Kiesling, Fae Ng, Thu-Huong Nguyen-Vo, and Daniel Torday.

The most generous writing community I have ever been a part of, the Randolph College MFA, with special thanks to my mentors Clare Beams, Mira Jacob, Julia Phillips, and Maurice Carlos Ruffin. And Gary Dop and Christopher Gaumer, so thankful for your shepherding.

PEN America, the Robert J. Dau Foundation, Tin House, Visual Arts Center of Richmond, and Voices of Our Nation (VONA).

The editors and publications who first saw something in these stories and helped share them with others: Karissa Chen at *Hyphen Magazine* and *The Rumpus*, Kyle Lucia Wu and Michelle Lyn King at *Joyland*, Leah Johnson at *Catapult*, Yasmine Belkhyr at *Winter Tangerine*, and Yuka Igarashi, editor of *Best Debut Short Stories: The PEN America Dau Prize 2017*.

The writers, scholars, and friends whose work, accompaniment, and care have helped me grow over the last decade—Kersti Francis, Rose Heithoff, Lena Barnard, Cynthia Schemmer, Lawrence Lan, Sumiko Braun, Katie Zanecchia, D. Arthur, Jenny Tinghui Zhang, Luca suede Connolly, Onyew Kim, Jeni Prater, Evan Mallon, LM Brimmer, Amanda Torres, Maura Wilson Schneider, Isha Camara, Rodrick Minor, Hannah Grieco, Talea Teasley, Sayuri Ayers, Margaret Malone, Tierney Oberhammer, and Emilly Prado.

My family—Stacie, John, Tera, Scott, Ian, Eliza, and all the Yews, Reeves, and Canessas—especially my grandmothers, Norma Yew and Terry Reeve.

My great-aunt Virginia Lee, for being such an important part of my literary lineage.

My sibling, Cory.

My southern, queer, and trans beloveds, who, I admit, are woven in and out of these stories. Thank you for being my muses and my people—Bradley, SH, Lee, Graciela, Vic, Sessa, Steph, Amanda, Dane, Crystal, Shelby, Beth, Diane, Jen, Collier, Raelyn, Micky, Luca (again), Rose, and so many others. I hope this book proves to deserve you.

Scout.

And, of course, again, my big love—Ace. Thank you for our beautiful life.